THE HIDDEN ROOM

JENNIFER SARASIN

SCHOLASTIC INC.
New York Toronto London Auckland Sydney Tokyo

Cover Photograph by Don Banks

ISBN 0-590-33104-3

12 11 10 9 8 7 6 5 4 3 2 1   6   4 5 6 7 8/8

CHAPTER
1

THE sound of squealing brakes and the lurch of the bus coming to a halt woke Claire suddenly from a dream. What was it? Yes, of course, the stagelights shining, the audience applauding, the hot, bright feeling of being a performer at the center of things. And then, something had happened to spoil it — what could it have been? Claire sighed and closed her eyes briefly, trying to recapture the dream, but it had vanished.

"Where are we?" she asked her seatmate, a young, tired-looking woman with an infant in her lap.

"Lee, I think. Yes, the driver said Lee."

"Oh, my gosh! That's me. That's my stop! Wait a second!" Shaking off the haziness of sleep, Claire Allenton grabbed her carryall and stumbled over the young woman, apologizing as her long, slender legs collided with the baby's tiny ones. Her khaki pants were creased and rumpled after the long drive from Suitland, Maryland, all the way to the Berkshires in western Massachusetts.

"Don't pull out — oh, please wait!" Claire gasped in the deep, husky voice that had always assured her of a good part in the school plays. That and her dark, vivacious beauty and, as her father never failed to point out, her unquenchable enthusiasm. If there was a theater around, Claire wanted to be a part of it — much to her parents' dismay.

"All right, young lady, I'm not going anywhere," the driver grinned as she jumped down to the ground. "But if you mess up my schedule, I'm reporting you to my company."

"I'll take full responsibility," Claire giggled, dragging her two big suitcases from under the bus's storage area.

"Looks like you're staying for a while," the driver commented, shutting the metal hatch with an emphatic thud.

"The whole summer. I'm an apprentice at a summer-stock theater in Becket," she confided proudly.

But she was puzzled to see the driver's cheery smile fade from his face like a secret message written in invisible ink exposed to the sunlight. "That Blairmore Castle?" he asked hesitantly.

Claire nodded.

"Gives me the creeps," he said shortly. Then he turned on his heel abruptly and climbed back aboard his bus. "Good luck," he said in parting. "You're gonna need it."

"Nice to start off on such a positive note," Claire muttered under her breath, lugging one of the suitcases up onto the raised sidewalk. She watched the bus pull out with a kind of annoyed smirk on her face. Nothing could dampen her spirits today — certainly not a sour bus driver. Probably just the fact that Blairmore was an ancient Scottish castle that had been moved to Becket stone by stone made some people think it was strange. That driver was probably the kind of person who always stayed in plastic new Holiday Inns when he went on vacation — never a charming old country inn.

Claire picked up the second suitcase and her carryall and settled herself on top of her first bag to wait for someone from the theater to pick her up. Lee was a comfortable-looking town, she noted — not cutesy quaint like so many others they'd passed through in this part of Massachusetts. But then, the area hadn't yet been invaded by tourists, since it was only the first week in June. Yes, Claire decided, her parents would like it here.

"We'll come to visit in July — give you time to get settled," her mother and father had promised when they put her on the bus with a few dozen hugs and kisses. Aside from a brief stint at camp when she was ten — a two-week horror show of noisy girls, too many mosquitoes, and a lot of boring sports — Claire had never been away from her parents for more than a weekend. She wasn't sure how she felt about that. On the one hand, she knew she'd miss them terribly. She was closer to her parents, especially to her father, than any of her friends were to their folks. But on the other hand, Claire had been longing for adventure and excitement for the longest time, and home was no place to find those two elements.

Someday she envisioned herself taking the really big plunge — moving to New York City to be a real actress.

But at sixteen, summer stock would at least give her a taste of genuine, professional theater. She knew her folks secretly hoped that she'd come to her senses and go into law or medicine or something practical, but they were smart enough not to tell her she couldn't try it. Actually, her father had helped her get this job.

"Didn't you once tell me you had a friend who ran a summer theater?" she'd hinted broadly to him one evening several months ago.

"Yes, Sean — Sean Latham and his wife. It's in an old, converted castle. No, wait, don't tell me," Richard Allenton had nodded with mock desperation. "You want me to call him and tell him I've got Sarah Bernhardt here, right?"

Claire had hugged her father appreciatively, loving him all the more for reading her mind. "Just tell him I'll work the lights or build sets or clean sinks or anything — as long as I can be near the roar of the greasepaint."

It had taken her parents only an hour to decide to make the phone call to Sean Latham. ("Let her get it out of her system," her mother had grumbled.) But in truth, she knew her daughter had a will of steel. Once Claire set her mind to doing something, it was as good as done. And what could the Allentons do but try to ease the way for her?

So Claire had her summer job all lined up — only $200 plus room and board in the castle — but still, a job in the theater! Well, maybe she *was* a little starry-eyed about the prospect of becoming an actress, but wasn't she entitled to be just a bit giddy under the circumstances? And then, to top it off, her parents had given her the best going-away present. As she was climbing aboard the bus, her father had quickly looped a necklace around her slender neck — it was a gold heart on a chain of seed pearls.

"Oh, Dad, Mom, thank you! I'll never take it off — not even onstage," she had exclaimed. "It'll be my good luck charm."

And even now, sitting alone on her suitcase on this busy street in Lee, miles away from home and everything familiar, Claire felt warm and loved as she touched the precious heart. It was part of her — a talisman that would guide her and watch over her.

"It's gotta be you. Is it you?" A voice just behind Claire made her jump up, and her suitcase toppled into the street.

"I guess," she nodded, shielding her eyes from the bright sun to look into the stranger's face. But the glare prevented her from making out any more than a well-defined silhouette. "I'm Claire Allenton," she went on. "Are you from the theater?"

"Kim Dresden." The young woman put out a graceful hand and shook Claire's forcefully; then she picked up one of Claire's bags and pointed. "That's the company truck. I'm the only actress in the world who can drive it, too. Hop in."

As they passed into a shadow, Claire glanced at the other girl's face and a tiny twinge of envy passed through her. Kim was so beautiful — a breathtaking blonde about three or four years older than Claire with long, neatly plaited braids and perfect features. Not a speck of makeup was necessary to enhance the actress's looks, nor did she use any. But she seemed completely unaware of her effect on others. The plaid shirt and patched jeans she wore spoke of a casual, comfortable person. Claire decided at once that she liked her.

"All set?" Kim demanded, slamming the rickety door on the driver's side of the truck.

Claire grinned and nodded, bracing herself as Kim put the machine in gear. This didn't help, though. She was practically thrown to the floor as the truck lurched up the street.

"Better than a bucking bronco, isn't it?" Kim yelled above the roar of the old engine. "I keep telling Sean it's going to kill someone someday, but he just rubs his hands gleefully and asks who I'd like done in."

"You're kidding," Claire said, her attention caught by her first glimpse of the rolling Berkshire hills.

"Yup, I am — but he's not," Kim giggled. "I warn you, honey, you may regret ever having taken this job."

"Oh? Why?" Claire asked, feeling uneasy for no specific reason.

"Because Sean Latham is a madman! A loon!" Kim threw her hands up in the air for emphasis, and the truck veered to the left. She quickly grabbed the steering wheel and righted their position in the road. "He's a workaholic and demands that everyone else has to be, too. He'll work your fingers and the rest of you to the bone and won't listen when you cry for mercy."

They were out of the town now, bumping their way along bright country roads. The vista opened before Claire like curtains parting on a stage — the green hills laid out as the backdrop, and flat farms and neat white-and-red houses as the scenery. A whiff of new-mown grass blew through the open window of the cab. The two girls caught it at the same time.

"Heaven!" Claire sighed.

"Not exactly, but it'll certainly do," Kim concurred, looking over at her passenger with a quizzical smile. "This *has* to be your first job."

"How'd you guess?" Claire was somewhat abashed. She must look as green as the grass out there.

"Just a hunch. I'm very intuitive. Are you old enough to drive?" Kim asked.

"Sure," Claire answered hotly.

"Okay — don't get all worked up. I only hoped we could split the chore. There are lots of odious things to do at a theater, and fetching and carrying is one of them." Kim turned the truck onto a bumpy dirt road. A leafy bridge of trees covered them, but did not manage to block out the bright sun.

Claire licked her lips, wondering how close they were. It was odd, but the air seemed to have changed subtly. She could feel — what was it? — a silent presence beside them. *How silly!* she thought suddenly. She was just such a city kid that a country road seemed substantially different.

"You worked at the theater last summer?" she ventured.

"Nope." Kim shook her head. "I did a show this winter with Sean in Chicago, and he invited me here for the summer. As you can see, *ingenue* sticks out all over me."

"You're lucky," Claire sighed. There was practically always one role for a pretty young blonde in most plays, which meant that the girl who fit into the ingenue, or "sweet young thing" category would always work. But given Claire's height and her dark, unusual good looks, she would undoubtedly have to wait until she was old enough to be a "leading lady" type before she really worked a lot in the theater. Or so her high school drama coach had warned her. Claire, however, wasn't the type of girl who heeded warnings. She just took her chances and plowed ahead.

"You'll like the company, I think," Kim was saying. "There's me — and knock on wood, you *must* like me! — and Sean and his wife, Stephanie, who's the leading lady, of course. A little weird, but you know, that's to be expected. Then there's the heartthrob, David Donnelly. Boy, he could play Romeo to my Juliet *any* day. Or should I say any night?" She stopped to glance at Claire and noticed she was blushing.

"Sorry, sweetheart — I forgot you're of a tender age. I was just joking. David's a Method actor, and they're poison from the word go. Anyhow, the housekeeper, Mrs. McLeod, allows no hanky-panky. Besides, we're roommates, you and me."

"Really?" Claire smiled warmly at this. As an

only child, she'd never had a roommate. It sounded like a nice idea.

"Wait'll you see our room. It's charming — sort of like a tomb."

"What?!" Claire felt that odd sensation again.

"Oh, never mind me. I'm just superstitious. But Blairmore Castle is awfully old and it's got a lot of ghosts hanging around, which gives the place a certain mood, if you know what I mean."

"What fun!" Claire clasped her hands in anticipation, only partially believing that Kim was serious. But her laughter was cut short as the truck barrelled out from under the trees and the landscape changed. There was a barren plain to their right, and off in the distance a large, gray shape loomed on the horizon.

"There she is." Kim pointed. "That's the castle."

No sooner had she spoken than the sun was whisked behind a bank of clouds, as if pulled by an unseen hand. The sky was suddenly dark and threatening; there was an odd odor in the air — of must and decay.

Kim pumped hard on the brake, slowing them to a crawl. "Kind of spooky, isn't it?" she said, shuddering.

And despite herself, Claire had to agree that it was. The gray stone shape materialized like a dream vision from the gathering fog. Each turret became defined as they approached slowly, and Claire could see the massive battlements ahead of them. The castle was gigantic — there seemed to be dozens of different wings grouped together around the main keep. As they drove closer, the huge front portcullis came into view before them. A large iron gate, it could be lowered to prevent entrance — or escape.

"At least there's no moat with alligators in it," Kim sighed. "Honestly, every time I drive out of this place, I swear it'll be the last. But I keep coming back — just a glutton for punishment."

Claire was awestruck by the power and majesty of the building. She couldn't take her eyes off the ramparts and the turrets that rose beside them. A wide parapet circled the crown of the castle — perfect for midnight strolls, she thought excitedly. Aloud she said, "I've never seen anything like it."

"It *is* pretty impressive. Some old coot — Alan Craig, his name was — brought the whole thing over from Scotland almost twenty years ago. It seems there'd been a fire, a terrible one. People were killed and everything. Gruesome, really. The place would have crumbled into ruins if Craig hadn't decided to move it to America and restore it. He died a couple of years ago, right here in Becket."

"Looks like the kind of place that would be perfect for hide-and-seek," Claire commented.

"Or something. Well, it is huge. There's plenty of space for the theater, the shop, the prop and costume rooms, a few dining rooms — one of them has an after-theater cabaret — and of course the sleeping quarters for cast and crew. And there are vast areas that nobody ever uses. I don't think Sean's ever been up in the tower."

She pulled the truck onto the long drive that led inexorably to the front gate. They were now too close to see anything but a wall of gray stone before them. Claire looked at it thoughtfully a kind of respect growing in her for this impressive piece of architecture. It had a stillness, a kind of watchfulness, as if it had a life of its own and could wait eternities for release from its stone promise.

I shouldn't be afraid — it's just a building, after all, she thought. And it wasn't fear, exactly, that she felt, but an anxious expectation. Something — she didn't know what, but something — was in store for her here.

"Home, Jeeves," Kim giggled as she pulled up to the tall, carved wooden doors, which swung open in a kind of greeting as the truck pulled to a halt. Claire jumped down from her side, practically knocking over the small, wiry man who had just rushed out from inside the castle. He had coal-black hair flecked with gray and a deep tan. His neat salt-and-pepper moustache gave him a dignified air, despite his paint-spattered workclothes.

"Claire! Claire Allenton. You look just like your father. What a resemblance." The little man stared up at Claire with almost frightening intensity. He gripped her hand and then shook it hard, continuing to stare at her with those bottomless eyes of his.

"Hello, Mr. Latham," she said shyly.

"Sean — please call me Sean. Welcome! Kim, take her things." The theater director began to lead Claire toward the front doors where a statuesque woman in a long white dress was waiting. She was even taller than Claire, and her impassive face never changed as they walked toward her. This was Sean's wife, Stephanie, Claire surmised. She was more handsome than beautiful, with a commanding presence. Claire had the feeling that the woman could read her thoughts and emotions — and that, even on first meeting, she was mistrustful of both.

But before they reached her, Stephanie turned and vanished, as if she didn't want to be bothered with anything as banal as an introduction.

"Stephanie?" Sean called after her, but there was no answer. He shrugged and smiled nervously at Claire. "She's out of sorts today. Bad news this morning. Well, you can meet her later."

He led her through a long, stone entrance hall to an archway that divided the public area and box office from the staff quarters. The smell of mustiness was overcome by the flowers that sat in a huge, colorful arrangement next to the placard announcing the first play of the season — an original mystery by Sean Latham.

"I didn't know you were a writer, too," Claire commented as they passed the poster.

"Oh, my dear," said a voice. "He does everything. Quite the Renaissance man."

Claire looked up to see an elderly woman sitting and knitting in a window seat at the end of the long corridor. She looked quite contented, as if she'd been transplanted with the castle when it was moved to America and had grown comfortably into that particular chair.

"Mrs. McLeod, you better watch your eyes," Sean cautioned her, walking briskly ahead of Claire. "The light's awful."

"What can I do?" the round, cheerful little woman sighed. "That Ryan promised to rig me up some spotlights over here for my knitting, but the boy's mind is elsewhere. What good is having a lighting director who won't give me any light? No good at all. And who are you?" she asked Claire, her fingers flying over the shiny metal needles.

"This is Claire Allenton, our apprentice for the season. Claire, this is Mrs. McLeod, our housekeeper," Sean noted. "Without her, there would be no theater," he went on dramatically, waving his arms in the air. "No meals, no order, no nothing. And now," he said in the same breath, "let's get you settled. You're rooming with Kim — I guess she told you." He didn't look at her as she turned to say good-bye to Mrs. McLeod, but kept walking at his own quick pace. As soon as he noticed she wasn't beside him, however, he turned back, his eyes two glowering coals of fire. "Well, what are you waiting for? We haven't got all day," he snapped.

Claire moved at once, completely dumbfounded by his critical reaction. She'd only paused for a moment and he'd yelled at her. That confirmed Kim's description of him — impatient, intolerant; in short, the typical director.

"I — I'm sorry. See you later, Mrs. McLeod." She raced after Sean, hearing her footsteps echo wildly on the flagstones. The place was a little dark and creepy, she noticed as she hurried along, and it certainly was the perfect setting for the murder mystery they were going to mount. But why, she wondered, was it so difficult for her to look at this castle for what it was — just a collection of stones, a neat jigsaw puzzle that housed a theater. She kept attaching other meanings, other qualities to it.

Yet as she walked more quickly down the corridor after Sean, she had the weird feeling that someone was watching her. No, it wasn't a feeling — it was a fact. Someone — or something? — she wasn't sure. Each chink in the walls appeared to move as she moved, as if the castle itself had eyes. Willing herself to keep going, Claire marched stolidly down the hall.

"Sean?" she called, but the still air bore no response. He had disappeared, and Claire was alone.

CHAPTER
2

CLAIRE turned abruptly into the next corridor, listening for the even patter of Sean's quick steps. She collided with a thud against a strong, muscular body.

"Ooph! I'm terribly sorry, Sean." But it wasn't the director. This was a stranger, a younger man with fierce hazel eyes and chestnut hair that curled in wild profusion around his head.

"Why don't you watch where you're going?" he demanded angrily. He walked past her and broke into a run, as if determined to get as far away from the source of annoyance as quickly as he could.

Claire stood there for a moment, feeling left out and uncomfortable. If theater people were this unfriendly, she wasn't sure she was going to get along. She stayed where she was, trying to get her bearings. Let's see, the corridor turned left and there was light coming from a window down there, so . . .

But before she could move, Kim came marching around the bend.

"Where've you been? Sean told me you'd be waiting in the room."

Claire, really glad to see her roommate, gave her a big smile. "He sort of abandoned me. And then I ran smack into this really angry-looking person —"

"David — that's the Method actor I told you about. He probably was just working on a scene in his bizarre mind. Don't worry about it." Kim linked her arm through Claire's and led her to the room at the end of the hall. Then, as if she could read Claire's mood, Kim gave her hand a squeeze. "You'll get used to them," she offered consolingly.

The room was as big as a dormitory and would have accommodated ten beds, but it was chilly, as though the sun had never touched it. There were two modern beds and dressers at the far end of the room and a professional makeup table with its bank of lights. A tiny clerestory window let in what little natural light it could.

"Ryan's promised to get us a couple of fresnels to cheer the place up — ah, those are stage-lights," Kim added when she saw Claire's puzzled expression. "But Ryan's always busy with something."

"I know," Claire smiled, feeling privy to a little company gossip. "Mrs. McLeod told me."

"So you've met the old hawk," Kim nodded. "Don't believe what she told you — Ryan's great. He just gives her a hard time occasionally. No, don't unpack now," she told Claire. "Unless my nose deceives me, it's lunchtime."

She cupped a hand at her ear and listened,

counting softly under her breath. A distant gong sounded once, twice, three times. "Lunch, as you can see," Kim said grandly, "is an all-star production. For dinner, the MGM lion roars. C'mon before it's all eaten. Actors are cannibals!"

The actor's dining room was just as Claire imagined it, having already seen a representative sampling of the castle rooms. A medieval mead hall would have had such a dining room — the long table stretched on and on, easily accommodating the twenty or so people seated at it. Sconces glittered from the walls — not authentic ones; these were electric — but they gave the appropriate effect. The cast and crew, however, a chattering bunch casually dressed mostly in jeans and T-shirts, seemed to have wandered in from the wrong century.

"Oh, sit here, dearies! I love to be surrounded by pretty women!" crooned a funny, nasal voice. Claire looked down, puzzled, and then giggled when she saw who — or what — had spoken. It was a ventriloquist's dummy, neatly attired in preppy clothes, wearing tortoise-shell glasses. Next to it was a second dummy in jeans and a T-shirt, who spoke before Claire could get a word in.

"Aw, what do you know about women?" the rather dumpy-looking piece of animated wood asked his buddy. "Howard, you have delusions of grandeur."

"And you, Boko," retorted the fashionable dummy, "are a slob."

Kim and Claire couldn't stop laughing as they took seats on either side of the arguing pair and the seemingly quiet gentleman who held one dummy on each knee.

"Claire Allenton, I'd like to introduce Howard and Boko, stars of the evening cabaret," Kim said. "And this is Ben Clark, a good friend of theirs. Need I add, he's a ventriloquist?"

Claire, still laughing, extended her hand to the man. He was about fifty, nearly bald, with a fringe of gray hair and a calm smile. He was wearing dark glasses, although the room was certainly not brightly lit.

"How do you do, Claire?" he asked her in the pearly tones of a British gentleman's gentleman.

"Nice to meet you, Ben." She noticed with surprise that he wasn't looking directly at her as his hand remained motionless in the air, waiting for her to take it. The man was blind, Claire realized with a jolt.

"Dad, move the puppets, would you? Give us some room." A young man with sandy blond hair and a huge bunch of keys at his waist straddled the chair beside Claire. He was very muscular, as though he really cared about keeping his body in shape. Claire decided he probably worked out with weights in his spare time.

"Hi," Claire said, smiling.

"My father actually thinks these sticks deserve seats at the table — can you believe it? Ryan Clark," he introduced himself brusquely. Then he dug in with relish, taking bread and cold cuts from the heavily laden platters on the table.

"The lovely thing about Howard and Boko," Ben countered, "is that they are children who never disappoint."

"Yeah." Ryan looked disgruntled for a moment, wondering if his father had just insulted him. Then he shrugged. "So you're the apprentice," he said to Claire. "Sean says you'll be doing a little bit of everything."

"That's right." Claire didn't really have her bearings yet, and it was dizzying to meet so many new faces so quickly, but she knew deep inside that it was important to be there. The confusion would pass in time. She looked around, taking in the feel of the hall and the people. "I'd love to learn to hang lights," she said.

Ryan appraised her carefully, his deep set gray eyes narrowing. He seemed to be judging her abilities and her character at the same time. "We'll see," he nodded. Claire had the feeling that for Ryan Clark to approve of you, you really had to be something special.

The rest of the afternoon was a blur of more people, more excitement, and more things Claire had no idea how to do. Professional theater bore scarcely any resemblance to the high school drama club, and it was kind of upsetting to have been such a big cheese at school and such an insignificant novice here. But if there was one thing Claire excelled at, it was digging in and trying hard. She was no shirker, and she intended to learn anything and everything about the theater by the time the summer was over.

By eleven o'clock that night, though, she was completely exhausted. Lots of the actors and crew had retired to the Green Room to read or play cards, but all Claire wanted was sleep. She bid the others good-night and started back down the corridor toward her room.

But probably because she was so tired, Claire made a wrong turn. She tried to retrace her steps, but only got more hopelessly lost. Undaunted, she kept walking, hoping to come to a familiar landmark, like the dining hall or the cabaret.

There was a wrought-iron winding staircase directly in front of her, and with only a moment's hesitation, she began to climb. Claire had wanted to get up on that parapet, and what better way to begin this new adventure of a summer job than to climb to the summit of the castle, as if she were a conquering hero and this was her goal.

The stairs led upward, ever upward in dizzying succession. Claire didn't look down once. There must have been several hundred steps, but she hurried up them, scarcely stopping for breath. At last, just when her legs were beginning to give way, she reached the top. Pushing hard at the old rickety metal door, she emerged into the night.

It was pitch black, with only a pale glow of a moon in the sky. It was so quiet, she could only hear the rustle of birch leaves in the breeze. The night was balmy, starless, and the air smelled as old as the castle. There was something eerie about being alone up here — Claire was so high up, she was on a level with the thick clouds that fogged the landscape ahead of her.

She breathed in the atmosphere, the ancient, mysterious life of the castle that seemed to swallow her up, even as she stood there. She wondered about the people who had once inhabited this place, long ago in Scotland, before she was born. But she wasn't afraid, even now.

Then she heard it. A muffled sound, like someone dragging something heavy. She turned and peered into the darkness, but was unable to make out any shape other than the turret opposite.

"Who's there?" she called, all her good resolve melting. Fear crept over her like a slithering snake, choking the very breath from her lungs.

There was no answer. The dragging sound stopped for a moment, then started up again, closer this time.

"Ryan, is that you? David?"

Nothing. But she heard someone breathing now.

"Kim, don't play around," she said, struggling to keep her voice calm. But now that was impossible. She didn't understand this terror that gripped her, making her feel somehow out of control, wildly wishing to flee — even if the only escape was over the side of these high gray stones. "Somebody, say something," she begged, sobbing with fear.

"Who told you you were allowed up here?"

Claire jumped because the voice was right by her elbow. "You scared me! Why didn't you say something?"

He was about her age and height, and now she could see that the object he'd been dragging was a large armchair. His light eyes glistened in the dark. From what she could see, he was very interesting-looking. He also reminded her of someone.

"Nobody comes up here but me," he said rather peevishly. "As far as I know, no one's allowed up here."

"Well, if you can be here, I can too," Claire said defensively, feeling ashamed and embarrassed for letting him spook her. "Why is this your private province?"

He exhaled deeply and didn't answer. "You're with the theater, aren't you?" he asked.

"Aren't you?"

"No way. I'm a cub reporter on the Becket Bugle. And my name is Ed," he said, his voice softening somewhat. "Ed Clark."

"I'm Claire Allenton." Grudgingly, she smiled, wondering why her heart was still pounding. "Are you Ryan's brother, by any chance?" she asked, when once again he was taciturn and silent.

"Half-brother. Ben's my dad."

"I see." She noticed his face now, a mercurial pattern of shifting emotions. She could tell that he was curious about her, but at the same time, he was slightly indignant about having his privacy interrupted. "Look," she offered honestly, "I wouldn't have even been up here if I hadn't gotten lost. It's my first day, see, and this place is sort of hard to figure out."

"That's okay," he sighed. "Have a seat."

She did as he told her, nestling into the plush upholstery and staring up at the night sky. They were both silent for a while, and then Ed said,

"I'm living in town with the editor of the paper and his wife. The Beckmans."

"Your dad doesn't mind that you aren't staying here?"

"Nah. Well, you know — different worlds. The theater's everything to him and nothing to me. He and Ryan travel a lot now, and I get to be on my own, which I like. I guess you could say I'm a loner."

"I see." Claire couldn't fathom what he was thinking. He seemed to be holding back as much information as he offered. She also didn't feel comfortable that she hadn't told him anything about herself yet. "I love the theater, but my parents feel the same way you do about it. I guess they're nervous about my getting hooked. So I'm reserving judgment until the end of the summer. This is my first real job, you see."

He looked at her keenly in the dim light, and their eyes locked in interest and something that approached respect.

"How come you don't like the theater?" she asked curiously.

He didn't answer, and she could see him debating whether he should share secrets with someone he'd just met. Then, after a long pause, he began to speak.

"My dad started in the circus about a hundred years ago in England. Married a bareback rider when he was really still a kid. But after Ryan was born, she skipped out, leaving Ben with an infant. Nice, huh?"

"Not very." Claire wanted to ask so many questions, but she kept quiet and let him go on.

"So he got married again — it was too tough managing by himself. My mom was an actress. She died when I was a baby and Ryan was about eight. Well, as you can imagine, Ben was in worse shape then. Two kids, and only a lighting director's salary, which wasn't much sixteen years ago."

"Lighting director?" She sat up straighter. "But Ben's —"

"Before. That was before. Listen, I gotta go," Ed said abruptly. "I'll see you. Uh, leave the chair. I come up here most nights anyhow."

And then, before she could even say good-night, he was gone and Claire was alone once again in the black silence. She sighed and wrapped her arms around her knees, hugging all her thoughts and musings into herself.

What an odd guy, she almost said aloud. It was hard to think of being close to one's family, and Ed seemed so defensive about Ryan and Ben, not to mention about the profession they loved and he hated. Or was it something else he hated?

She shrugged and stood up, stretching out the kinks. It would undoubtedly be a long, hard day tomorrow and she was exhausted, after all.

Once down the winding stairs, Claire somehow found the right corridor within moments, and from there, getting to her room was easy. As she turned the ornate brass handle, she wondered fleetingly if Ed was home in Becket yet — and when she'd seen him again.

"Where've you been?" Kim yawned as Claire walked into their room. She was brushing out her long golden hair at the dressing table by candlelight, looking like a vision from a movie.

"Up on the roof — I mean, the parapet," Claire said, beginning to undress. "I was talking to Ryan's brother, Ed. Kim, did you know that Ben used to be a lighting director?"

"Hmm? How could that be?"

"Well, naturally it was before he was blinded." Claire looked at the other girl thoughtfully.

"Gee, that's sort of awful." Kim shuddered slightly. "I mean, it's not as if he had a career he could hold on to, like Stevie Wonder or something." Then, putting down her brush, she threw herself on the near bed. "I'm beat," she sighed. "And I'm really shaky on my first-act lines. Would you mind very much cueing me tomorrow before rehearsal, Claire?"

"Be glad to." She reached into her cosmetic kit for her toothbrush and soap dish, but she wasn't watching as she did so. The whole kit toppled to the floor, spilling items everywhere. A small pocket mirror that had been buried at the bottom crashed on the flagstones, shattering into dozens of pieces.

"Oh, no!" Claire wailed.

"How could you do that? A mirror — oh, Claire!" Kim was out of bed in an instant, her nightgown balled up in one hand as she dashed across the room.

"Move aside, you're barefoot," Claire commanded. "Kim, I'll get it. It's just a little mirror."

"Seven years bad luck!" Kim wailed. "How could you?"

"Don't tell me you're superstitious," Claire

25

laughed. But she could see for herself that Kim's dismayed expression was real. Still, Claire was positively dumbfounded to see her roommate pick up the dressing-table chair and smash it down on the large glass shards, pulverizing them into a fine dust.

"What are you — what in heaven's name did you do that for?" Claire demanded, suddenly uneasy about her roommate. Had Kim said that *Sean* was mad? Maybe it was Kim who didn't have all her marbles.

"It might fix it," Kim said nervously, backing away from the pile of powder that sat in a silvery pool beside the bureau. "It's said that if the shards are crushed so that no mortal can ever see his reflection in them again, then you don't have all that bad luck to contend with. Or worse, a death in the family within a year."

Kim looked up at Claire and, seeing the strange look in her eyes, she laughed anxiously. "Okay, so I'm a little wacko. I'm just terribly superstitious. Always have been. Maybe it's all a lot of hooey, but I believe it. So forgive me?"

"Of course, silly." Claire smile half-heartedly.

"Now leave that and go to bed. I'll get a whisk-broom in the morning and clean it up." Kim scurried back to her bed and drew the covers up.

Claire was more than a little shaken, but she attributed it to her exhaustion. *If I can just drop off quickly, I know I'll be fine in the morning.* But as she climbed into bed, she found her eyelids fluttering open, refusing to let her sleep. A catalogue of faces and names and sights ran through her mind — the approach to the castle, Sean and

Stephanie, Ben's dummies, getting lost, being terrified by Ed and then, this mirror business. If all this had happened to her at home, she would probably have shrugged it off and forgotten it, but here at the castle, everything seemed magnified, larger than life.

At last her thoughts became hazier, and she could feel the lethargy of sleep dragging at her arms and legs, willing them to give in and relax. She was halfway there when she was jolted awake. A woman's high-pitched, silvery voice, raised in anger, seemed to be coming through the wall.

"Did you say something?" Kim asked in a whisper.

"That wasn't me." Claire pressed her ear to the wall, and now she could make out two voices. A man and a woman, arguing. "Is Sean and Stephanie's room near ours?"

"No. They're on the next floor, at the opposite end of the wing. Shush." Kim got out of bed and crept across the floor to Claire's bed. The two of them listened intently, peering at the wall as if it might offer them an X-ray vision of what lay beyond.

"What *is* behind here?" Claire asked.

"Nothing. The corridor ends. There's no room on the other side." Kim shook her head. "I've been here a week now and it's been totally silent every night." She sighed, listening again. In a minute, since they had heard nothing, they backed off and looked at each other quizzically.

Kim grimaced. "We couldn't both have imagined that at the same time, so it must be ghosts. Remember I told you this place practically burned to the ground years ago? Well, somebody's spirit must be hanging around from that awful fire." Slowly, she walked back to her bed and climbed under the covers.

Claire settled back against her pillow, biting her lip to hold back the panicky laughter that threatened to burst out of her. Her shaking hand rested lightly against her throat, counting the quick beats of her pulse. In a few seconds, it was back to normal — a nice, steady rhythm — and all she felt beneath her fingers was the gold heart on its pearl chain. As she held it, warm memories of home flooded over her once again. So what if mirrors broke and ghosts spoke through the walls? Her necklace was her good luck charm, and would protect her.

I'm getting as superstitious as Kim! she thought in annoyance, closing her eyes. *It's just stupid — I don't need any protection, because there's nothing to be protected against.*

But even after she drifted off to sleep, that high silvery voice haunted her dreams. When she woke in the cool, gray dawn, the nightclothes tangled around her sweating body, she knew with a dead certainty that there was something evil in this castle. She only prayed that it wasn't interested in her.

CHAPTER
3

THE first person she saw as she walked into the dining hall was Ed. In the early morning light, she could see that she had misjudged him the previous night — he wasn't interesting-looking, he was gorgeous. And the smile on his face as she walked toward him with her cup of coffee made his strong features even more appealing.

"Well, hello," he nodded. "Join me?"

"Thanks," Claire responded shyly, putting her cup down and taking a seat beside him on the long bench.

Kim staggered toward them carrying a tray laden with food. "You're not plunging into theater life on an empty stomach, I hope. You" — she pointed at Claire, — "eat! Hi, Ed, how's things?"

"Just fine." He was rather cool with Kim, Claire noticed. Was that because she was a "theater person"?

"You never eat with us," Kim pointed out, her delicate mouth filled with sugar doughnut. "Must be the enticement of new blood."

Ed blushed and looked away, and Claire gave her roommate a warning look. If there was anything she hated, it was someone trying to fix her up. Clearly, Ed felt the same.

"Or maybe it's because he wanted to see his family," Kim added cheerily, waving at Ryan who had just entered the room with David. "Look who's here," she called, motioning Ryan to come over and join them. He and David took coffee and toast from the serving counter and came over to the table.

"Hi, little brother." Ryan casually ruffled Ed's hair. The expression on Ed's face was that of a skittish deer about to bolt, Claire noticed.

"Hello, Ryan." Calmly and purposefully, Ed stirred more milk into his coffee. Claire wondered again about his standoffish behavior. When she'd come in, he was smiling broadly. But as the others joined them, his mood had become subdued, even sullen.

"I've just about got that first act licked," David was saying to Kim. "I worked on it all last night, and I think I've cracked it. The motivation for the murder isn't anger, see, it's all got to do with the guy's relationship with his mother, and I can relate —"

Kim stifled a groan and threw Claire a meaningful look. "Darling," she said, patting David's hand, "don't give me that psychological analysis junk, please. The reason your character kills my character is 'cause that's how Sean wrote it, period." She popped a piece of coffee cake into David's open mouth. "I cannot abide weirdos talking about their mothers," she said adamantly.

David's eyes flashed. "Now, just a second! I have had the finest theatrical training in the country and —"

Ryan stuck two fingers in his mouth and sounded a long, piercing whistle. "Cut it out, you two. Claire's going to think this whole acting company is out of its mind. And she wouldn't be too far off, right, little brother?" he asked Ed.

Ed was silent, and his blank expression remained fixed.

"Well, anyway," Kim went on, "if you're going to run lines after midnight, David, you should ask me instead of whoever you got. That girl in the box office — what's her name? — sounds positively awful when she yells through the walls."

"What do you mean?" David frowned.

"Last night. You were rehearsing with someone. Claire and I heard you distinctly. And you sounded pretty bad together if you ask me."

"I wasn't working with anyone," David protested. "And what do you mean, I sounded bad?" The actor's arched nostrils flared in egocentric annoyance. Claire suddenly knew what her father meant when he talked about "those actors who are so stuck on themselves."

"Kim and I did hear voices last night," Claire confirmed. "It could have been anyone, of course," she added hastily.

"Aw, you guys'd fight over the number of times you get to walk onstage," Ed said in disgust, pushing away from the long table. "Why don't you grow up already? Ryan, where's Dad?" he asked brusquely, not even looking at Claire as he turned away. She suddenly felt like she had to make things all right again — everything seemed to be in such turmoil — but she didn't know where to begin.

"Haven't seen him," Ryan shrugged.

But at that moment, Ben entered the room. Claire was transfixed as she watched him negotiate corners, hardly hesitating as his feet took him surely and swiftly toward the table.

"My boy," he said, his face lighting up. He'd evidently heard his younger son's voice through the door.

"Hi, Ben. Just thought I'd come over to have breakfast with you, but now I'm late for work. Some other time, okay? See you tonight, Claire," he threw over his shoulder, getting out of the room as if all the furies were chasing after him. Claire could not figure him out. She did feel sorry for Ben, though. Clearly, he wanted more contact with his son — more than Ed would allow.

Kim pulled on Claire's sleeve, jerking her back to reality. "Would you run those lines with me now?" she begged. "Since David has some silent partner, he won't want to work with me."

"I *told* you —" he exploded.

"David, it's all right," Kim said sweetly. "Just keep it down tonight, would you? Claire and I couldn't sleep, you two were arguing so loudly."

"Kim, you're an idiot," David snorted. "I wasn't talking to anyone."

Ryan chuckled and shook his head. "This is a better mystery than what we've got onstage. 'Who were the two voices talking after midnight, and what were they saying? Tune in tonight and find out — if you dare.'"

"Two voices, eh?" Ben effortlessly spooned sugar into his coffee. "Naturally it must have been Howard and Boko. They were arguing something terrible last night. I finally gave up trying to play mediator and went to bed."

Claire looked at the man curiously. Did he really believe his dummies had lives of their own, or was this his understated sense of humor? She couldn't help thinking about Ben years ago, sighted, alone in England with two young sons. What a life he'd had — and how tragic that things had turned out this way. She thought of her own father with his comfortable life, his stable existence, his nice family, and she shuddered slightly.

"Let's move it, girl," Kim prodded her. "There's work to do — and Sean to contend with if we're late." She pushed back her seat and in doing so, knocked her coffee cup over on David's sleeve. The cup was nearly empty, so hardly any liquid spilled, but David reacted as though she had scalded him.

"What's the matter with you!" he yelled. "Why do you always have to mess everything up?" The room quieted down, everyone embarrassed by his inappropriate rage. He took no notice and simply stalked out the door, his head hunched down between his thin shoulders like a bantam cock about to go into the ring and square off against a bigger bird.

"He certainly has a temper," Claire muttered. She was troubled by David's excessive anger.

Method actor or no, he just didn't seem in control of his emotions.

"You said it, sweetie." Kim sighed and shrugged, motioning Claire toward the door. "The only thing to do is ignore him. C'mon, let's get a breath of air before rehearsal starts."

The girls bolted into the outer court, laughing as they jostled each other to get through the large medieval doors of the castle. The morning was lit like a stage set, with long fingers of filtered sunlight reaching out to touch the dew on each blade of grass.

"Magical," Claire proclaimed, throwing herself down on a patch of moss and taking the script from Kim. "I could sit here all day."

"No you couldn't. You better enjoy the outdoors while you can, my dear, because you're going to be shut up in that dark, dank old castle for eight long weeks. Start on page ten — I'm okay up to there."

Claire gave her the cue and Kim launched into her monologue — a comic explanation of how her character had come to live at Old Antelope Lodge. She hated the country, was allergic to everything, but her parents had insisted it would be good for her health. She got through the speech without a hitch.

"'Then you won't mind if I hang around, just until my wife shows up?'" Claire read David's character's line with a certain menace, imagining the actor even as she spoke.

"'Make yourself at home' — oh, yuk! That's where I go to the dresser and get the gun, right?" she asked Claire.

"Uh-uh. You've got three speeches before that. Take your time," Claire encouraged her. She thought of her drama club teacher, Mr. Slauson. He used to tell her that if she couldn't remember a line, she should try thinking about what her character really wanted and needed, and some approximation of what she was supposed to say would pop right out. "And to heck with the playwright!" Mr. Slauson always joked.

The clang of a cowbell made Kim jump. "That's us. Let's go — Sean's an ogre about lateness." Her blond braids flying, Kim grabbed the script and Claire's hand, yanking her along, back into the depths of the castle. The sun was shut out as the huge doors clanged shut behind them. Claire kept running, excited now and eager to start her first day as a real, professional apprentice.

The group — including Stephanie; David; Charlie Norton, the young second lead; two local women, Sue and Pennie, who'd been jobbed in to do small roles; and Emil, the older character man — was sitting haphazardly in the first few rows of the theater, listening to Sean, who sat on the apron of the stage, his short legs dangling. When the two girls rushed in, breathless, he frowned and paused.

"Didn't mean to rush you," he snapped sarcastically. "I don't suppose either of you ever heard the old saw about the show must go on?"

"Yes, sir, I have," Claire piped up, and the whole cast burst out laughing. She was so horribly embarrassed, she wanted to crawl under the stage.

"That was just a rhetorical question, dummy," Kim hissed at her. "Keep your mouth shut and listen."

Sean took a deep, theatrical breath and continued with his blocking instructions for Act One. He asked Stephanie, who hadn't been cast in this show so she could have ample preparation for her starring role in the next production, to take the rest of the cast to the back of the theater and run scenes with them. Then he told Kim and David to get up onstage.

"And you, Claire," he said in a kinder voice. "You hold book — that means you're the prompter. Don't give these two any lines they don't ask for, but jump right in if they've really gone up — that means blanked out."

"Yes, sir," Claire said nervously, walking up and taking the book with sweaty palms. She felt as though everyone in the room was watching her.

"After rehearsal, you go to the costume shop with Kim," Sean continued. "Maggie Evans is going to be fitting everyone today, and I told her you'd take down measurements for her."

"Okay."

"And when you're not doing anything else, you can go on back to the kitchen and get us all coffee." He lit another cigarette and took a deep drag. "That's five black, three with milk no sugar, one with three sugars no milk. And however you like yours." He looked at her closely. "Got it?"

"Yes," she lied, feeling smaller and smaller. She was like Alice in Wonderland, just having glugged down the bottle that says, DRINK ME and having unhappily shrunk to White Rabbit-size. There was so much to do, far too much to remember.

"Sit in the wings and watch!" was Sean's last instruction to her. He gave her a hand to get up onstage and then he jumped off the apron. Kim gave her a sympathetic wink as she wandered back behind the first downstage curtain to the rickety chair just close enough for the actors to hear her if they needed a line.

Ryan was sitting on the floor cutting colored gels to fit on his Kleiglights. "I heard all that," he scowled. "The guy doesn't know when to stop."

"Well, I have a lot to learn," Claire acknowledged, trying to keep one ear on him, one on Kim and David, and her eyes on the book.

"If you get a chance this afternoon, I'll take you up on the catwalk — how about it?" he offered, his gray eyes mild and calm. He pushed his unruly shock of hair to one side. "Not afraid of heights, are you?" he asked, pointing up to the top of the theater where the majority of the lights were hung from a narrow, slatted ledge.

"Not me," Claire grinned.

"Then you're on," he whispered, his fingers still busy with the mat knife. She realized that he didn't even need to pay attention, so practiced was he at cutting and fitting.

" 'Then you won't mind if I hang around, just until my wife shows up?' " Claire heard David give the line. Then there was silence. He repeated it, an edge to his voice.

"Oh, fudge!" Kim grunted. "Claire, what is it?"

" 'How long did you plan to stay?' " she read in a loud, firm voice. Kim took the cue and kept going, leaving Claire the brief opportunity to look around. With half a mind on what was happening in the scene, she glanced behind Ryan toward the set pieces waiting in the wings, the loaded prop table, filled with items that ranged from a fake hot-fudge sundae to a bayonet. There was a smell to the backstage area that made Claire giddy both with remembrance and expectation. Old musty costumes became knights and princesses; the painted canvas flats stretched over two-by-fours, redolent of glue, became whatever was pictured on them — a world in a tiny frame. Claire was in love with the feeling of being there, of being part of it all.

"Now when you leap for the gun, Kim," Sean was saying when Claire's attention returned to the scene in progress, "I don't want anything emotional happening between you. David, be as cool as you can — no expression at all. Kim, you're just protecting yourself — it's survival. Remember, you don't get killed until the next act."

"Right. I know. That's why my Act Two lines are so easy to remember," she said dryly.

"But the point is that you try to tell everyone that he's dangerous up till the very moment of your death, and nobody believes you. That's what makes it really scary."

The cowbell clanged, indicating time for something new to happen. Claire assumed — or hoped — it was a coffee break.

"Just a second — don't move," Sean commanded. "Kim, go for the gun like a baseball player. Slide into home plate." He leapt up onstage in one graceful bound and flung himself toward the prop gun on both knees.

"Sean, I can't do that — I'll pop a kneecap," Kim protested.

"Sure you can. Relax and lean back. Take the weight on the balls of your feet. Your knees don't hit till the end."

"Sean —"

"Do it!" he told her fiercely. David looked on, a satisfied smirk on his face.

Clumsily, Kim repeated the move. She didn't quite land where Sean wanted her, and she fell over in a heap before recovering, but she did reach the gun.

"All right, Miss Baryshnikov," Sean muttered. "Practice that till you get it right. Wear long pants. Break time." He waved his hands and the other actors who'd been working with Stephanie in the back of the theater scattered.

"Not for you," Sean told Claire and Kim. "Get over to costumes."

"Some taskmaster," Ryan grumbled from the wings. "Hey, Claire, come find me later."

Claire nodded, grateful that someone was actually taking an interest in her and didn't just see her as an insignificant go-fer.

Kim walked back into the wings, cursing under her breath. "Directors, honestly! You can have 'em." She led Claire to the winding wrought-iron staircase at the back of the stage-left wings. "This is how we get up to the stage from the dressing rooms," she explained. "Costume shop's right down there. Go on . . ." She glared out into the house where everyone else was lounging around enjoying their coffee and then, still muttering, followed Claire down the stairs.

They were not prepared for what greeted them at the bottom.

"Oh, God!" Kim scuttled back up four steps, dragging Claire by the sleeve.

Claire felt her stomach drop, as though she'd gone down too fast in an elevator. Lying stretched out on the floor before them was a dressmaker's dummy wearing a simple full-skirted sundress. A pair of shears protruded from the left breast of the mannequin. A party hat with a red streamer sat at a cockeyed angle beside the form, its brim smeared with stage blood.

"That's my costume." Kim could scarcely breathe. "I saw the designer's sketches." Her hands were shaking as Claire took them.

"It's just a silly prank. Someone's idea of a joke. See, the dress is hardly torn at all," Claire said, not believing a word that came out of her mouth. "Let's find Maggie — is that her name? She'll probably have some explanations."

But it *was* creepy, Claire couldn't deny that. And what was even more bizarre was the way Kim kept staring at the mannequin — as if she saw herself in that dress, impaled with those scissors.

"Go get Sean, bring him here," Kim said weakly. Then, as Claire watched in amazement,

Kim darted down the last few steps, placed her right foot squarely on top of the open scissor handles and then bent to yank them out of the dressmaker's form.

"Kim, leave them there — don't you want Sean to see —?"

"Bad luck," Kim moaned. "Don't you know the only way to avert it is to step on the scissors and then pick them up?"

"No, I didn't know," Claire said in exasperation, taking the scissors and placing them back on top of the dummy, over the slash in the dress. "But I do know you're too superstitious for your own good, Kim. You just tampered with the evidence." She was annoyed with her roommate's childish behavior, and yet, she was herself more scared than she wanted to admit. Trying to take charge, she pulled Kim back up to the wings and, not letting go of her hand, she walked her centerstage, peering through the bright downlights out into the house.

"Sean, would you come here, please?" Claire said in a tone he couldn't ignore. She might be the new kid on the block and the lowly apprentice, but she was in better shape than Kim, who was still shaking.

"What is it? I told you two to go to work with Maggie." But he jumped onstage and came right to Kim, embracing her as though she were a frightened child. "Sweetheart, what happened?" he asked.

The other actors, David and Stephanie among them, were right behind Sean and the girls as they retraced their steps down toward the costume shop. Stephanie went directly to the hat and picked it up.

"Who did this?" she asked. Claire suddenly realized that this was the first time she'd heard Sean's wife speak. Her voice was deep and uninflected, like a stream rushing over pebbles. "This is horrible! I won't stand for it." She turned and faced the group. Her eyes took in every one of them, as she searched for something that would give away the culprit.

"The scissors were right here," Claire said, pointing to the rip in the garment.

Sean righted the dummy and carried it under his arm to the costume shop. The door was shut and the light was out.

"Guess Maggie finished her work for the day and went home," quipped Bob Lynch, the set designer.

"Why don't you mind your own business?" David was at Kim's side, his arm around her protectively as Sean threw open the door of the costume room and the others trooped inside. He pulled the chain of the overhead light bulb and the room took shape for Claire. The costumes, their hangers neatly labeled with the name of the actor who would wear them, bore silent testimony to Kim's terror. There, on her hanger, was a child's party dress decorated with tucks and ribbons. It was torn to shreds, almost beyond repair.

Kim wailed and ducked under David's arm, escaping out the door and up the stairs. Claire wanted to go after her, yet her feet remained planted to the floor.

"Okay, who's the joker?" Sean asked.

"Don't be stupid," Stephanie snapped at him. "No one in the company would do such a thing. It must be one of the local kids. I bet he crept in through an open window, or something."

But the room, if anything, seemed impenetrable to Claire. There were no windows at ground level, and only narrow chinks farther up the walls. She eyed Stephanie suspiciously, wondering if she was jealous that her husband hadn't written a leading-lady part in this, the opening show of the season. Did she want Kim's role, and was she trying to spook her so she'd quit?

Oh, stop thinking like Dick Tracy, Claire told herself sternly. *There's got to be some logical explanation.*

They were all standing around anxiously when a small, round woman in her early fifties burst through the doorway. "Oh, Sean, I'm sorry I'm late. My car wouldn't start and I —"

Maggie Evans, the costume designer, stopped and stared at the torn child's dress Sean was still holding. She didn't have to say a thing. Claire could tell just by looking at her that she was as frightened as everyone else.

"But I don't get it." Ed sat in the niche of one of the great turrets, listening to Claire's story. "It had to be some kid's prank, right? It's a dumb thing for anyone around here to do. And counterproductive. The show opens on Friday."

"How can you say it's dumb? It's sick." Claire shook her head and paced some more. The day had been exhausting and she really wanted to go to bed, but she was certain she'd never sleep. And she'd looked forward to seeing Ed all day, sure that he could give her a sane, untheatrical appraisal of what had happened.

"Look, there's lots of weird stuff going on these days. A lot of kids don't care about messing up other folks' property. Anyhow, the general population of Becket, Mass. thinks actors are, shall we say, bizarre. . . . They're outsiders. Or maybe some critic thinks Sean wrote a lousy play — who knows? Just forget it."

"But I can't. Oh, you're so exasperating." Claire frowned at him, annoyed that he was taking the whole thing so calmly. She hardly knew him, and yet she needed to talk to him — really *talk*, not just chat. It occurred to her that she never had that problem at home. She could always go to her father's study at the end of the day and confide in him. They understood each other, even if she couldn't talk to her mother. Here, though, she didn't know if anyone understood her. Also, she didn't know who to trust.

She sighed and got up to leave. Maybe things would look better in the morning.

"Hey."

She felt Ed take her hand and it sent a shiver through her. Not of fear, though — of pleasure.

"Don't blame me for this, would you, Claire? I'm just an innocent bystander."

"You do hate theater, though," she said.

"Only because of what it did to my dad. I don't go around sticking scissors in dummies or cutting up dresses."

"I never said —!" Claire pulled away, even

angrier that he'd taken her exasperation at his not understanding as an accusation.

"I know. Look, we may come from two different worlds, but we can still be friends, can't we?" he asked simply. "It may take us a while to learn to communicate, but I think it might be worth it."

"Well, sure." She was flustered, but flattered, too. It was hard to assimilate everything — her anger, her fear, her attraction to this boy.

"Sleep on it, why don't you." Ed waved her to the door. "I'll be around if you need me."

She nodded and walked slowly to the winding staircase. She could feel his eyes on her. "Goodnight."

"Good-night." He sat there in the dark for a long time after she left.

Claire crawled into bed as soon as she got back to the room. She was suddenly aware of Kim's presence in the other bed, her shining hair kissed to a silvery sheen by the moonlight that streamed in through the casement window. Too tired to count sheep, Claire closed her eyes, willing her breathing to get deeper and heavier. She was almost dozing when she heard it — that high-pitched woman's voice, first laughing, then sobbing wildly. The sound went on for only a few eerie seconds. Then there was silence.

"Sticks and stones can break my bones, but ghosts can never hurt me," Claire muttered. Even so, she clutched her gold heart tight in her fist and held it as she might have held her father's hand, if he were there beside her.

Sometime before dawn, she fell asleep.

CHAPTER
4

THERE was too much to learn over the next five days — about people, about theater, about herself and her abilities — for Claire to spend any time worrying about voices or scissors stuck through mannequins. This was repertory summer stock, which meant a week to mount the first show and then the following week to rehearse the second show while the first played at night. There would be two more plays to work on for the second half of the season, as well as a children's theater show, in which Claire would finally get to act, for Saturday matinees.

During that first dizzying week, Bob taught her how to stretch canvas on wooden frames, staple it tight and then wash it with the foul-smelling size, or glue, that pulled it skintight as it dried overnight. The flats, as they were called, were then painted as scenery. Ryan taught her to rig the flashbox she would run in the second act of the murder mystery; Sean taught her the most efficient way of running a rehearsal; Kim taught her makeup; Ben showed her how he talked without moving his lips — but Claire couldn't for the life of her learn to do it.

She and Kim tried to forget the awful incident with the costume, and didn't discuss it between themselves or with anyone else. As for that nighttime woman's voice, it was silent. Maybe the ghost had gone on vacation, Claire thought hopefully.

Every evening, pooped but too happy to sleep, Claire would sit with Ed high above the castle on the dark parapet and talk. Since that night when she'd implied he was too cold-blooded, he had loosened up with her and she had grown more comfortable with him. They didn't speak of her fears again, nor could she bring herself to ask him about Ben or the accident that had blinded him, but they found enough to talk about that mattered. Ed was so *normal* — he didn't call Claire "sweetheart" and "darling" the way the actors did; he didn't boast about his accomplishments in a grand, theatrical manner. Instead, he told her his dream of being an investigative reporter, and about how excited he was that his editor, Mr. Beckman, was going to let him write a column every once in a while. Also, Ed was interested in her. Claire could tell that by his keen, probing questions and the way he listened, so calmly and understandably, when she talked. Maybe her father was right, Claire thought. Maybe there *was* life outside the theater worth knowing.

On Thursday, the day before dress rehearsal, everyone was word-perfect. All that needed doing was polishing up cues and smoothing out rough spots, like Kim's slide across the stage. As Claire worked with Ryan up on the grid, handing him C-clamps so he could focus the lights, she could hear Kim groan every time she fell on her knees. Even though Sean had consented to let her rehearse wearing kneepads, she had them off now because they would show under the light sundress — which Maggie had completely repaired — that was her first act costume.

"You wish you were out there, don't you?" Ryan helped Claire down the last rungs of the ladder and jumped down to stand beside her. He noted the wistful expression on her face as she watched Kim hit the mark again, and curse the pain again.

"Oh, I do!" Claire suddenly realized how naive she sounded and she turned to him with a self-deprecating laugh. "You think acting's silly, just like Ed, don't you?" she smiled.

"Silly? No, that's not the word I'd use." Ryan shook his head. "Well, listen, if you want it bad enough, you'll get what's yours by right. In the meantime, why don't you get down in that trap and let's try out the flashbox. Hey, everyone," he called to the group, "we're running cue 25, in case you're interested."

The rest of the cast and crew moved offstage, some to the wings and some out into the house, to watch the explosion Claire was about to trigger.

She climbed down through the small hatch in the stage floor. It was barely big enough to accommodate her lanky body, but she folded herself neatly in half and concentrated on mixing the half teaspoon each of potassium nitrate and magnesium with the mortar and pestle Ryan had given her. Then she wedged the bottom of the trap open, placed the mixture in the flashbox, and gave Ryan a sound cue as she jumped clear of the hatch, down to the prop room below the stage. The box was ignited electrically from Ryan's light board. Claire heard the bang practically beside her, although of course she was about half a football field away when it went off.

"How'd it look?" she asked, scrambling up the stairs to the backstage area.

"Gorgeous!" Sean enthused. "Ryan, I like it, keep it just like that."

"Yes, sir!" Ryan winked at Claire and she nodded back, feeling very much like a pro. More important, she felt accepted and appreciated.

"Okay, everyone, take five — or ten — whatever," Sean told the exhausted cast. Only Stephanie looked well rested, but of course, she hadn't been working like a dog all week. "As a reward for all your wonderful cooperation and exemplary performances," Sean grinned, "I'm allowing you to take in Ben's early show at the cabaret tonight. As you know, this is the first night the public will be let into our lair, so be on your best behavior and wear appropriate clothing — no bathing suits or fright wigs, please."

"I'll wear my fangs," Ryan whispered, and Claire giggled.

"Boko and Howard — and Ben, of course —

have worked very hard to get their act in shape," Sean went on, "so I know you'll give them all the encouragement you can. Okay, get some rest. We start again after lunch. Kim, you better put some makeup on those knees."

Kim grimaced and hobbled out of the theater, followed by David and Stephanie.

"You go ahead, get some lunch," Ryan told Claire. "I'll finish up by myself."

"Sure you don't mind?" Claire almost offered to stick around, but she knew she couldn't keep her eyes open another minute. After the technical rehearsal the previous night, she'd stayed up with Ryan, Bob, and Maggie till nearly 3 A.M. doing last-minute odds and ends. She didn't want lunch; she wanted a nap, so she went straight to her room and fell onto her bed.

If Mrs. McLeod hadn't rung the cowbell right outside her door, she would have slept right through the afternoon. But luckily, she was roused at once, because Sean had a variety of chores for her. She did them without complaining, but without much enthusiasm, either. By 6 P.M., when they finally stopped for the day, she was barely functional.

"Maybe you ought to skip the cabaret," Kim said as she started to dress for the evening half an hour later.

"Are you kidding?" Claire scoffed. The girls had raided the costume shop and selected two elegant gowns to wear that night. Claire's was deep burgundy velvet with long sleeves that ended in a point below her wrist. The skirt was narrow and hugged her slim figure. Kim's dress was an aquamarine Southern Belle confection of organza and lace. "I may fall asleep on my feet, but I'm gonna be there." She kicked her grubby jeans unceremoniously under her bed, too tired to pick them up. "Anyway, I told Ben I'd set up the chairs for him. What a nice guy," she mused, wrapping herself in her terrycloth robe and starting for the shower.

"He is," Kim agreed, "but I think those dummies are creepy."

"What do you mean? They're just wooden puppets."

"Yeah, you and I know that, but Ben treats them like they're real. A bit bizarre, if you ask me." Kim shrugged, checking herself for any flaws in her appearance. Naturally, there weren't any.

"That's just his sense of humor," Claire said. "He doesn't believe they're actually talking." She had spent enough time with him over the past week to be pretty certain of this. Although it was true that he did talk to them when he didn't think anyone else was around.

"You better rush, kiddo," Kim declared. "I'll meet you at the cabaret," she sang out on her way out the door.

Claire took a nice, long shower, luxuriating in the hot water and the silence. As she stood under the warm blast, she imagined what the evening might be like — her walking into the room, Ed being wowed by her dress, Ben giving a brilliant performance, Ed actually spending time with his father after the show. At least, that's what Claire hoped would happen. There were so many things to hope for and dream of, Claire thought as she dried herself off and began to dress. You could make a life out of hopes and dreams and never see reality at all — something her mother often accused her of doing. Then her father would jump right in and defend her, of course, and they'd somehow be paired up against her mother without even meaning it. Her father really liked the fact that she had an imagination, maybe because it was something her super-practical mother lacked completely.

Why was she suddenly thinking about her parents, she wondered as she stepped into the glorious red dress and closed every tiny hook and eye. Maybe it was Ed and Ryan and Ben that brought all this to the forefront. And maybe, she thought ruefully, maybe it was just plain old homesickness.

"Go out and knock 'em dead," she told her tall, regal image in the mirror. She drew a comb through her dark curls, slipped into her black flats, and dashed out of the room at precisely seven-thirty.

Down the long, echoey corridors she ran, no longer afraid of those feelings she'd had about the castle during her first few days here. Naturally, no one was watching her — it was ludicrous to even have dreamed that. The place was old, and old places seem threatening sometimes before you get to know them — that was all. As Claire crossed the hallway and stepped out into the public part of the castle, she smiled at the walls that had once frightened her. But that was before she became an insider, part of the very theater itself as she was tonight.

The cabaret was nearly full, since opening week at Blairmore was always a big deal in Becket. Local townspeople were serving coffee and sandwiches to tourists and relatives at the various tables; the theater people sat together clannishly at one big table in the corner. Then there was a hush as Ryan, from the light booth, set the houselights halfway down.

Claire hurried toward the backstage area, grabbing two folding chairs as she went. Ben was standing quietly, listening to the buzz of the crowd and preparing himself. He looked positively elegant in his top hat and tails, and Claire smiled as she saw him.

"Do help me, my dear," he said, not even turning to her. Clearly, he had sensed her presence. "Now where did I put my cape?"

"Here it is. Sorry, Ben, I meant to get here earlier." She picked up the long black cape lined in red silk and draped it over his shoulders.

"All right, my boys. I do believe it's time." Ben's face looked so pale and white in the shadows, it was almost like a mask.

"You nervous?" Claire whispered.

"Goodness yes. Only an actor who's not worth his salt hasn't the sense to be nervous."

She looked around for the dummies and spotted them on the ledge that supported a makeshift prop table.

Claire did a double take, looking at Howard again. She could have sworn he was grinning at her! No, that was absurd, of course it hadn't moved. She could see now that its wide mouth just looked mobile in this dim light.

"Oh, my dear, would you let them know I'm ready?" Ben asked her, patting her hand. He bent down to pick up Boko, who was lying in a heap beside Howard. Howard was a model of sartorial splendor in an exact replica of Ben's costume. Boko, of course, was a mess in jeans and a T-shirt.

"Break a leg," Claire whispered, dashing out front to place the chairs and the small table with a glass of water on it. She swiftly moved off-stage, which was Sean's cue to do the introduction. He left the table where he was sitting with Stephanie and walked into the spotlight Ryan flashed on him. Claire darted over to an empty table in the corner and took a seat. She hadn't noticed Ed anywhere, but hoped she'd just missed him in the dim lights.

"Ladies and gentlemen, good evening, and welcome to the opening of Blairmore Castle's fifth season," Sean began, taking in the audience at a glance. "We all hope you're going to enjoy the shows — our first opens this Saturday, as I know you know, but I have to give it a plug anyway."

A ripple of laughter coursed through the room.

"But tonight, for your pleasure, direct from command performances in England and the U.S. of A., we present to you Benjamin Clark and Friends. They've asked me to ask you to sit back and enjoy yourselves. Thank you all, and we look forward to seeing you throughout the season."

The curtains parted just as Claire felt a hand touch her shoulder.

"What? Oh! Sit down," she motioned to Ed, who looked splendid in a black turtleneck and tweed jacket. His eyes took her in in one appreciative glance, then jumped to the stage. He looked nervous, and Claire assumed he was having stage fright for his father. He was probably anxious about how good Ben would be.

"Well, hello, hello, hello!" Boko waved at the people from under Ben's feet. He sat stage center with Howard perched on the chair above him. Ben picked him up carefully, lovingly, and put him on his lap.

"Benjamin," Howard said in a disgusted voice. "Would you kindly ask this lump on a log to leave us alone?"

"Oh, Howard," Ben chided, "how can I do that?"

"Who's calling who names?" Boko was livid as he jumped across Ben's knees in his attempt to get at Howard. "You're the one who's in the way."

"Why, you! . . ." Howard looked ready for a fistfight.

"Now, just a moment." Ben's voice overrode them. "This is not nice at all. Boys, there are people out there who've traveled miles to see you. They don't want to spend good money just to watch you two argue. Howard, why don't you sing the people a little song?"

"Oh, well, all right." Howard looked flattered.

"This I gotta see. Or do I mean hear?" Boko chimed in.

As Ben picked up the glass of water Claire had placed onstage, Howard burst into an off-key rendition of "Some Enchanted Evening." The audience gasped as the ventriloquist kept drinking and Howard kept singing.

"He's really amazing," Claire told Ed as everyone gave them a round of applause.

"I agree," Ed nodded noncommitally. "That's hard, too. He tried teaching me when I was little and I could never manage it. Ryan used to throw his voice all over the house, but I couldn't even talk with my lips closed."

"It's impossible," Claire whispered. "I tried it, too."

They were quiet as the threesome onstage told corny jokes and then took questions from the audience. Someone asked Howard where he'd been educated ("Harvard and Oxford, of course!") and David asked Boko where he got his wardrobe ("Wardrobe — what's that?"). Then Boko asked some elderly lady for a date, and the room exploded with laughter as Ben and Howard tried to dissuade him. The act ended as the three of them sang the Hallelujah chorus — not together, exactly, but overlapping lines so quickly that Claire could almost believe the dummies were performing solo.

"That was great!" she sighed as the audience filed out around them, laughing and talking.

"Yeah. Look, I won't be able to sit around with you tonight," Ed said, looking very preoccupied. "I've got a deadline — shouldn't even have come tonight but I wanted to see Ben. I really can't stay now, though." He looked like he was about to bolt out the door.

"You're not even going to congratulate your father?" she asked in annoyance.

"Ben didn't expect me to come. I'll see his show plenty of times this summer. I just can't hang around now." He was very flustered, his eyes darting to the door and back to Claire.

"You don't even like to acknowledge that he's your father, do you?" she said suddenly. It was none of her business, of course.

"What do you mean?" Ed's eyes narrowed, and she could feel the tightness in his shoulders.

"Ed, you hardly talk to him — or talk about him, for that matter."

"You're ridiculous. You know nothing about anything." He started for the door and then abruptly turned back, his face a mask of rage. "And if you want my advice, Claire, you won't stick your nose where it doesn't belong if you don't want to get into trouble."

"What? . . . What are you saying?" She wanted to go after him and demand an explanation, but she also wanted him to apologize. He was gone before she could decide what to do.

"Don't mind him."

She turned to see Ryan, who had clearly heard the whole thing. His calm features reassured her.

"What's wrong with that brother of yours?" she sighed as they walked out of the cabaret together.

"Wish I knew. Say, Claire, would you mind

57

testing the flashbox once before dress rehearsal tomorrow? I want everything to go smoothly." He walked away almost as briskly as Ed had, and Claire shook her head in frustration. People simply didn't act like this where she came from.

She looked around for Kim, but her roommate was nowhere in sight. Most of the theater people went out after shows to celebrate, so Claire figured that most of the staff was probably long gone by now. Only a few townspeople were standing around in the lobby, smoking and talking.

Feeling left out, lonesome, and piqued that no one had asked her if she wanted to come with them, Claire wandered back toward her room. The lovely red dress weighed a ton, and what good had it done, anyway? She peeled it off and gratefully climbed into jeans and a sweatshirt. Oddly enough, though she'd been exhausted all day, she wasn't tired now. She didn't feel like reading or writing a letter home.

"Might as well do the flashbox now," she said aloud. "Then I can sleep late tomorrow."

She closed the door behind her and padded down the hall to the stairway that led to the prop room. It was so quiet — *tomblike*, as Kim liked to say — but it felt all right to Claire as long as she talked out loud. It wasn't really as though she were talking to herself, she rationalized as she took the powders and the flashbox and climbed up onstage, flipping on the work light as she left the wings. No, it was just keeping herself company.

"Maybe I need a dummy of my own," she

laughed as she opened the latch in the heavy trapdoor. She didn't bother securing it. "If I had a dummy, we could talk to our heart's content."

She sat inside the tiny hatch and pulled the flashbox in after her. It was pitch black inside, so she worked quickly, mixing the ingredients just as she had done it a dozen times at rehearsal. She would have to ignite the box herself tonight.

"'Double, double, toil and trouble,'" she muttered, giving the powders a stir with the stick she'd left there for the purpose. She reached down to the bottom of the trap, feeling for the hook that opened it. The spill from the work light scarcely lit the flashbox itself, though, so she crawled all the way inside, squashed down like the bellows of an accordian.

"Oh, where *is* that thing?" She had her finger on the hook when suddenly the trapdoor fell over, hitting her back with a dull thud. "Ow! Damn!" she yelped.

She pushed upward, struggling in her awkward position with the heavy metal door. It wouldn't give an inch.

"Oh, no!" She remembered, too late, that she had neglected to secure the door open. Telling herself to keep calm, she reached below, fumbling for the lower door. She had the bolt now — all she had to do was slide it open and she could jump clear to the prop room below. Why wouldn't it move? It was almost as if it had rusted in place, or been nailed shut. She'd opened it easily just yesterday.

Beads of sweat covered her lip and her forehead, and it occurred to her that there wasn't much oxygen in this tiny hole. Barely enough to last . . . how long? An hour? The whole night?

Don't be silly. Someone will notice you're gone, she thought as her lips moved in silent prayer. This was no time to start talking to herself; she would use up too much air by doing so.

Carefully, she arranged her long legs under her, crossing them. Her head still bumped the top of the hatch, but at least she had room to maneuver her hands. She tried the top door until her muscles cried for mercy and her hair was soaked with perspiration, but she could only budge it an inch or two. It was almost as if something was lying against it. The bottom one was hopeless. No matter what she did, the bolt refused to give.

She closed her eyes in the dark, breathing evenly but not too deeply. Suddenly, for no reason, she thought of a game of hide-and-seek she'd played with the neighbor's kids when she was six. Sam and John were eight and nine, and they seemed to delight in torturing her. When she was "it," they'd found her and locked her in the cellar. Her father finally discovered her half an hour later, a shaking mass of anger and terror.

Now as she sat in this cramped hole, her right leg totally asleep and her left painfully propped against the damp wall, she had to remind herself that she wasn't a child anymore, at the mercy of some little boys' prank. This was serious. But was it an accident? Had she knocked over the door by brushing against it? And was she simply too freaked to be able to move the lower bolt? Rationally, practically, she went through every conceivable reason for her predicament. She kept coming up with the same answer.

Someone wants to get rid of me. A sob tore from her throat as panic took over. She beat against the door with her fists, screaming, "Help! Somebody please *help!*" And then the tears coursed down her face, and she couldn't speak anymore. She *was* a child again, and she was terrified.

Her sobs became muted, softer, and less frantic. She knew she had to conserve her energy. All she had to do was sit very still for a few hours and morning would come. That would mean dress rehearsal. The whole cast would be here by 9 A.M.

If she could last that long.

She rested her head against the upper door, trying to think of words to a Broadway show tune. That would keep her busy. And who knew how long it would take to go through the scores of all her favorite musicals? Just long enough. . . . Maybe she'd even doze off. . . .

No! She jerked herself upright, banging her head. She mustn't fall asleep. It would be like closing your eyes in a snowstorm and just letting nature take over. Whatever she did, she had to remain alert. That was the only way she'd last till morning.

She was certain she had started to hallucinate. She heard sounds, like footsteps over her, like the clang of steel on steel. How long had she been locked inside this trap? It seemed like days.

"Hello! I'm in here! Please, please!" She rapped on the door above her head with raw knuckles and winced. The footsteps stopped.

Then again, "Help! Somebody!"

There was the unmistakable sound of feet running closer, temptingly close to her. Then with a whoosh, the trap was pulled open.

Claire moaned and shielded her eyes from the dim stage light. Painfully, she raised one arm out of the trap.

"What the —? Claire, my God!"

Strong arms lifted her out and arranged her neatly on the floor. Through a hazy fog, Claire could make out a face. Then she coughed and kept on coughing. The air seemed thicker, denser, too much for her stifled lungs to bear.

"C'mon, kid." It was Ryan. He hoisted her up and draped her around his muscular body, practically dragging her out into the house and from there down the corridor and out into the fresh morning air. She never knew whether there were other people with him or whether they just appeared after she was taken outside.

Ryan deposited her on the grass beside the driveway and gently massaged her neck and shoulders. She gasped for oxygen, breathing like a fish out of water.

"What the hell happened to you?" he demanded, his gray eyes concerned and frightened.

"Got locked in. Tried flashbox last night.

Hatch wouldn't open," Claire choked.

"What is going on?" Sean with Stephanie behind him was standing over her. "You gave us a terrible scare, young lady. I hope you're aware of that!" He sounded more angry than sympathetic. But Stephanie bent down beside Claire and smoothed the bedraggled hair from her forehead. It was the first time Claire had seen Stephanie smile.

"You poor dear," she crooned, her perfume smelling wonderfully fresh and exotic this close. "Let me get you a cup of tea. Then bed."

"But dress rehearsal," Claire protested as an assortment of hands helped her to her feet. David was there and Kim, who looked positively white, and Mrs. McLeod, who looked her usual calm, unruffled self.

"Are you really all right?" Ryan asked. Claire had never imagined him capable of being this kind, this caring, as if her health and well-being really meant something to him.

"I'm . . . I guess so. I was really dumb, that's all. You told me to secure the hatch, and I didn't. I guess I had to learn the hard way." She was just a bit dizzy now, but she certainly felt better.

"Well, what are we standing around for?" Sean demanded as he glared at them. "It's show time, folks!"

Flanked by Kim and Stephanie, Claire walked slowly back inside the castle. She was grateful and relieved and happy to be alive — but she was also on her guard. *Who's responsible for my accident?* she wondered, *and how can I find out before something else happens?*

CHAPTER
5

E D was there when she woke up. She'd never been so happy to see anyone, so warmed and relieved to open her eyes and find him sitting at the dressing table, reading yesterday's paper over and over again.

"Hi," she said.

He jumped, then stumbled off the chair to get to her side. "Ryan called me, so I told Beckman I needed the day off. Are you all right?" His light blue eyes caressed her, and then his hand reached up and softly touched her face.

"I'm okay. I was just dizzy and tired — the sleep did me good."

He sat back and stared at her, as if seeing her for the first time. "Lord, you're brave. If I'd been locked in a box all night, I'd be a basket case."

"I was — for a while."

"Nah, not you. You're perfect." And with that, he leaned over and planted a kiss on her lips. At first, she drew back in surprise, but then, half-smiling, she came toward him and exchanged the gift he'd given her. Just the touch of his hand on hers made her shiver. The kiss sent goosebumps up her spine.

"Thanks for coming to see me," she said softly.

"Want me to stick around for a while?"

"Well, sure, but I'm getting up." She knew she could confide in him now. He was an ally.

She swung her legs off the bed, suddenly realizing she hadn't even bothered to undress before collapsing. "Listen, Ed," she said, "something's very fishy here. I know you're going to tell me I'm paranoid, but —"

"No, just terribly theatrical. Hey, if you feel well enough," Ed smiled, "maybe you ought to get over to dress rehearsal. I know they need you."

"I will, I will, but I have to talk about this." Claire was suddenly annoyed with him, because he was trying to distract her. "I think I was locked in there because somebody wanted to scare me. I think Kim's dress was tampered with for the same reason. Someone's up to no good, Ed. And you're the investigative reporter, so you've got to help me."

Then Ed did something that turned her blood cold. He patted her on the head as though she were an idiot child and pushed her back toward the bed. "You could use a little more rest. Now I want to see you all gorgeous and fully recovered at opening night tomorrow. That a promise?"

She exhaled slowly. "I'm fully recovered right now, thanks. And I'm going back to work. You might as well do the same." She stalked past him, out the door, feeling awful in a way because he did like her and he did care enough to come and see how she was. But he was also patronizing and condescending and, what was worse, he wouldn't believe her!

As she wound her way down the halls and through the corridors to the theater, she wondered whether maybe she was going just a little overboard. After all, who could she suspect? Sean might have a devious enough mind to write a murder mystery, and he might be a taskmaster, but he was an old friend of her father's. Stephanie might be jealous of Kim, but what could she have against a young apprentice who wasn't even in the show? Then there was David. Of course he was weird, but *that* weird? Bob Lynch was too busy being tech director and stage manager; Ben and Ryan were the sweetest, kindest people around; and Kim —

She stopped dead at the door to the backstage area. Could Kim have planted the scissors in the dummy? She had had ample opportunity to get down to the costume shop before rehearsal. And Claire hadn't seen her after the cabaret. She could have been waiting in the wings, waiting to lock Claire in the hatch. But why? And what about that woman's voice through the walls? Could that be a tape recording?

Her mind was still doing flip-flops when Sean came up behind her. "You're up," he commented. "How are you, for heaven's sake?"

"Good. Really. I better get to work." Act Two was already running, and David, as the crazed killer, was just about to strike Kim with the breakaway chair. Claire steeled herself to turn away from the scene, to tune out Kim's very realistic scream. Of course, Claire now felt that scream deep down inside, where her own worst fears lived. Fears of loss, of loneliness, of being the only one who knew something bad was happening, even — though she'd never consciously thought of it before — fears of death.

Then she turned back to the prop table and concentrated on what she had to do. The show, as she had heard over and over since she first fell in love with the theater, must go on.

The dress rehearsal was over at four-thirty, and Sean called everyone into the house for notes. They'd have another technical run-through the next morning, but the evening was free for rest and relaxation. And sleep, Claire thought gratefully as she sat with Ryan going over the light-board plot. She would have to run the last-act lights here every other night when Ryan worked the cabaret, setting up for Ben's show.

"How're you doing?" he asked when Sean dismissed them a brief five minutes before the dinner gong.

"I'm fine. I was pretty mean to your brother today, though. And after he took the morning off to come see me, too."

Ryan laughed. "Ed's got thicker skin than a crocodile — always has. What'd you do to him?"

"Well, I was trying to explain that my getting locked in the trap was no accident — just as Kim's dress wasn't. He wouldn't believe me when I told him somebody's been tampering with —"

"And why should he?" Ryan asked sharply.

"Claire, you don't know a whole lot about professional theater yet. Don't question what you can't understand, okay? You'll get along a lot better."

Claire sighed and shrugged, vowing as they walked into dinner together to say no more about her suspicions. She'd have to find out by herself what was going on. It was as simple as that.

But she had no time that evening or the next day to do any sleuthing, because preparations for opening night took up every second. She ran into town with Kim to get fresh flowers for the lobby, picked up cases of beer and soda for the cast party afterward, helped Ben to dress Howard and Boko for the great event, and heard Kim's lines until she knew them backwards. Even in the dressing room that evening, Kim was still practicing. The other two women in the cast, who were locals with small parts, eventually got tired of hearing her and walked out, leaving Kim and Claire alone.

Claire had worn her black jeans and black turtleneck, the conventional costume for all stagehands who weren't supposed to be seen by the audience during scene changes. But she'd brought along her peach silk blouse to wear to the cast party, and she hung it next to Kim's costume on the hook. As she chatted, trying to keep Kim's mind off her stage fright, she would stop occasionally to listen to the guys on the other side of the wall. The men's dressing room was back-to-back with the women's.

"Go out to the wings and check the house,"

Kim demanded, putting rouge on her high cheekbones. "Please," she added.

"You want an accurate head count," Claire joked, "or you just want to know if your mother came?"

"Oh, go on!" Kim practically pushed her to the door.

Laughing, Claire sped up the steps to the wings where Ryan and Bob were taking turns at the hole that had been cut in the curtain precisely for this purpose — so the cast and crew could get a look at the audience.

"How is it?" Claire whispered.

"Full house! Packed." Bob grinned, his nearly bald head shining in the downlights.

"Great. Kim's about to have a heart attack." She raced back down the stairs, so happy and excited, she felt like singing. Instead, she whistled a silly little tune she made up on the spot.

As she opened the dressing room door, the whistle died on her lips. "What is it?" she asked hoarsely, looking at Kim's face. It was gray, despite her makeup.

"Was that you?"

"Well, yes. I —"

"Don't you ever . . . never again, do you hear me? Do not *ever* whistle backstage. Not if you want the show to close — or something awful to happen to one of the cast." Her hands were tightly clenched in front of her, and her voice was so shrill, David and Sean had come around from the men's side to find out what was going on.

Kim pointed a shaky finger at Claire. "Get her out of here. I don't want her near me. She's a jinx."

"But I —" Claire struggled to explain herself. "I was only whistling."

"That's bad luck, Claire. Every actor knows not to do that backstage," Sean said, shaking his head.

David glared at her. "I don't know why you ever came to this theater," he growled. "You've done everything wrong since you got here."

Claire wanted to cry, but of course she couldn't — and wouldn't. "I'll get out of your way. I've got a lot of work to do," she said staunchly. She walked out of the room, her head held high, telling herself that after all, she wasn't used to any of their peculiar rituals or bizarre superstitions. *They* were the weird ones, not she.

She took refuge in doing everything perfectly that night. As the show progressed, she performed every set change, took every light cue, as though her life depended on it. She hardly watched the show at all, but simply and mechanically performed her duties. It made her forget that she was still an outsider — a kid who didn't understand the rules and regulations of adult life. Whenever her mother criticized her for being too spontaneous or too frivolous or too — something — she would always say, "Claire, you'll be a child for life." That was just how she felt tonight.

But when Bob rang down the final curtain and the cast assembled behind it for their curtain call, the cheers of the crowd made Claire forget her own problems. She might almost have been out there herself on that stage, covered with glory and claiming her reward. There was nothing in the world as satisfying as an audience who loved you.

Bob yanked on the rope again so the group could take another bow, and Claire sighed happily, walking behind the set to stage right where she had to put her prop table in order before her job was finished for the evening. Ben was sitting quietly in a corner with his dummies, a contented smile on his face.

"What're you doing here?" Claire asked as she placed the stage gun in its case. "Shouldn't you be over at the cast party?"

"Can't stay away from *this*, you know," the older man grinned. "My, does this take me back. Opening night, the adoration of those out front. My dear, once the theater's in your blood, you can't escape it."

"I feel that way, too," Claire admitted.

He pushed up his dark glasses and rubbed the bridge of his nose thoughtfully for a minute. "Did you know I worked here years ago, when Blairmore Castle stood on Scottish soil?"

Claire turned slowly and peered at him in the darkness. "You're kidding! You mean before Alan Craig moved it to America? You were in the theater before it burned down?"

"Oh, my dear, for a good deal before that," he sighed. "Those were the good old days! What a place Blairmore was. Set amid the moors, heather all round, the crowds coming for miles, from as far away as London, in fact. It was said that Princess Margaret and Anthony Armstrong-Jones used to meet for romantic weekends at the inn just down the road. They'd come to the theater, and then sneak off before anyone could see them."

"How romantic," Claire smiled. "Ben, do you mind if I ask, were you . . . were you in the fire? Was that how —"

But before she could get the question out, the cast and crew mobbed them both, making such a din that Claire couldn't even hear herself think.

"Party's starting!" Bob took her by the hand and Ryan took his father's arm, and they were both forcibly led down the steps from the backstage area. As they raced down the long halls and intricate corridors to the Green Room, Claire could hear the party already in progress.

Kim was busy flirting with David, silly with the evening's success. David didn't crack a smile, of course. Mrs. McLeod appeared carrying a huge tray, and the other cast members paraded in with the drinks in huge tubs of ice. Relatives and friends swarmed the room, and in a moment, Claire had lost sight of Ben.

Somebody put a stack of records on the old Victrola, and before she knew what was happening, Claire was dancing, swooped up by a local kid she didn't even know. It didn't really matter that she hadn't had time to change into her nice blouse — she was suddenly laughing and spinning, and nothing counted except having fun.

"I'm cutting in," said a firm voice, and there

was Ed, facing her. The other boy grumbled and shrugged, then turned away to find another partner.

"Still mad?" Ed asked above the din of the music and talking.

"Not possible," she yelled back.

"What? I can't hear you."

"Me either," she laughed and kept dancing.

They didn't stop for the next half hour when finally, exhausted and sweaty, Ed begged for mercy. "You need a Coke," he told her in a tone that would brook no disagreement. "I need about three."

He clasped her around the waist and drew her toward the food table. There were egg rolls and four kinds of dip with raw vegetables. There was spinach quiche and a huge turkey with all the trimmings. The cakes and pies went on for yards — and everything looked simply splendid, definitely good enough to eat.

Ed and Claire each filled a plate, took a soda, and ducked out onto the veranda where only a half-dozen other couples had retreated from the mayhem.

"I owe you an apology," Ed said when at last they could hear themselves think.

"No, I owe you one." Actually, this wasn't true, but Claire was feeling happy and generous tonight.

"I shouldn't have tossed off your scary experience like it was nothing, though," he said, "especially right after what you'd been through."

They were interrupted by the sound of a loud crash, and then, voices raised in anger. Quickly they turned back inside, only to see Bob and Ryan restraining David, who looked like he wanted to hit somebody.

"You little punk," he yelled at the kid who'd asked Claire to dance, "you say another word and I'll flatten you."

"You and who else," the boy barked sullenly.

Sean quickly escorted the boy out, but David still looked menacing. Just as Kim came over to take him away from Ryan and Bob, he wrenched free of the two men and picked up an empty plate, which he hurled after Sean and the boy. Luckily it fell short of its mark. Kim dragged him off before he could do anything else, and slowly the party got back into motion again. But the sounds of people having a good time were certainly muted now.

Ryan, spotting Claire and Ed, walked over to them. The three of them strolled back outside into the night air.

"I sure wouldn't like to get on his bad side," Ed commented.

"Nor I," Ryan muttered. "What a nut."

"What'd that kid say to him to get him so riled up?" Claire asked.

"Oh, you know, something about his acting. I didn't hear the whole thing."

Claire bit her lip, unsure of how far she should let her conjectures lead her. "I don't know that much about the Method," she said slowly, "but I do know that as an actor, you're supposed to bring your own reality — your own life experience — to your character. You're actually supposed to live the part. Do you think it's possible that David is getting carried away by playing a crazed murderer? That he's been acting out off-stage?"

Ryan laughed and ran a hand through his hair. "You're writing scripts again, Claire. David's harmless."

"Frankly" — Ed took her by both hands and made her look at him — "I agree with Ryan. The guy's got a temper, and maybe he's a little unstable, but I don't think he's turning into a killer. Be honest, Claire — you don't either."

She shook free of him and hugged herself, pacing the veranda and trying to think. "I don't know what to believe. But I'm scared." She turned and looked at the brothers, who seemed to her, in the moonlight, much more similar in appearance than they did in the daytime. "Don't either of you have any ideas?"

"Well, me," Ryan said, "I'm going to get another beer and enjoy myself. Lots of stuff I want to do tonight, and that includes eating and drinking my fill and finding any woman out there who can stand the sight of my ugly mug to dance with. Just as long as she's not a performer," he grunted, moving off into the crowd.

"What's he got against performers?" Claire asked curiously.

"Well, you know. His mother. Want to dance?"

"Your mother was a performer too. Do you resent everyone connected with acting because of her?"

"Of course not. C'mon, Claire."

"Ed." She stopped him with a hand on his arm. "Your father told me tonight he was at his theater when it was still in Scotland. Speaking of acting, I just wondered about him. Was that — was it when he was a lighting director? When he could still see?"

Ed cleared his throat nervously. "You hit it, Sherlock. Now do you want to dance, or what?"

"But," she said resisting his pressure on her arm, "what I can't figure out is why he'd come back to work at Blairmore. Why of all the theaters in America he'd go to this one — the very place where his life fell apart." She licked her dry lips. "Why is he here, Ed?"

Ed shrugged. "Returning to the scene of the crime? I don't know, Claire." When he saw her face, he quickly reassured her. "I was just joking. There wasn't any crime."

"Oh?"

"I think he really came here because . . . well, you'd have to ask Ryan about this, but I think it's like a homing pigeon coming home, or a salmon swimming upstream. I mean, it was a bad time for him in one way, but it was filled with wonderful memories, too. He loved this theater, and he loved the people connected with it.

"But when my mother died, he struck out for new lands, a new life. He took a boat over here and polished up his ventriloquist act on the way. He left me with the Beckmans in Middlefield — they were old friends of Alan Craig and would have done anything for him or a pal of his. So then Ben took Ryan and went on the road. From what I hear, Ryan was like his seeing-eye dog. Only nine years old and doing one-night stands all over the country. Ben taught him to throw his voice, and sometimes he'd do the act if Ben didn't feel up to it. Audiences thought it was a gas, a little kid with the two dummies. I guess Ben never wanted to settle down after he left Scotland. And I guess he did what was right for him." Ed suddenly realized he'd been talking a blue streak and stopped with an embarrassed laugh.

Then he said, "I only saw them when they happened to be playing New York or Boston. That's why we're not awfully close. And Ben seemed to be waiting for Alan Craig to open up Blairmore to the public. When Sean got hold of it, five years ago, Craig called Ben and told him to come on over, and he came running. Anyhow, Ben and Ryan were always too busy working to spend a lot of time with me. And meanwhile, living with the Beckmans, I got to be really tight with them. Now, they seem more like my family than my real relatives."

"But you must have resented being left with strangers," Claire said sympathetically. "I mean, Ben was your real father. *Is* your real father," she stammered.

"Yeah, legally he is. But I was too young at the time to resent anything — just an infant. And now I've got my own life, and I like it fine. So," he smiled, quickly changing the subject, "what do you think about rejoining that party?"

"I'm . . . would you mind very much if I copped out for the night? I'm so pooped I can hardly stand." She knew he wouldn't believe this — she'd been dancing like a maniac not half an hour ago. Still, she needed some time alone. She needed to put some of the pieces of this puzzle together.

"Well, okay. I guess you haven't gotten a lot of sleep lately, have you?"

She smiled, her dark eyes growing wider as she saw the tenderness in his face. He really cared about her — and she had to admit he was the first boy she'd ever known who made her feel like a person, not a silly little girl who didn't count. And yet there was something she had to do; something she couldn't tell him about.

"I think I've been up for two whole days, maybe. I've got tomorrow off, though, at least till three when we have a brush-up rehearsal."

"Great!" His handsome face broke into a smile. "Let's take a picnic and go to the falls."

"It's a date."

His fingers entwined with hers, then let them go. It was the nicest good-night. Claire left him in the Green Room and slipped through the doors before anyone could see she was out of the room.

Once in the hall, she padded down the long hallway, grateful for her black clothing that covered her like night's cloak. Now on her own, she was going to explore the castle. She was determined to get to the bottom of the mysteries — of the scissors in the mannequin, of the voices in the walls, of the locked trapdoor — even if it killed her.

CHAPTER
6

SHE would have to be very careful and consider every possibility. It was conceivable that anyone in the theater was responsible for the strange events that had occurred. It could be David with his weird temper; it could be Kim with her mania about superstition; it could be uncaring Sean or even — and this was the most awful possibility — it could be Ben. Why had Ed even talked about "returning to the scene of the crime" if he didn't know something about his father that he wasn't telling? And wouldn't a man who'd lost everything in a terrible fire be an apt candidate for instability?

Claire stayed close to the damp walls, starting down the corridor toward her room. It was so quiet now with everyone at the party downstairs, she could almost believe she was alone in this big, ancient castle. *If these stones could talk*, she thought with a shudder.

This is really dumb, was the next thing that occured to her. If there was a crazed killer around, she shouldn't be stalking him on her own. She should know that much from watching TV — the heroine always gets caught and nearly killed when she starts off on some foolhardy, daredevil mission. But who would she take with her? Ed and Ryan didn't believe her, and at this point, as much as she liked them, she just didn't know. . . .

A distant sound caught her attention and she stopped, flattening herself back against the wall. Footsteps far away, moving quickly, gracefully — a *woman's* footsteps, perhaps? Then, nothing.

Claire came out of her niche and as she moved, she heard that woman's voice again, the same one she and Kim had heard through the wall of their bedroom. It sounded like it was coming from somewhere over her head.

And then, suddenly, the pieces of the puzzle fell together. There was only a blank wall beside the room she shared with Kim, and no other space before the staircase to the tower. But suppose the wall was hollow? And suppose there was a room above it? Voices filtering down through that shaft would *sound* closer, as if they were coming from a room that connected to theirs.

A hidden room in the turret of the castle? One that nobody knew about except . . . except any one of the people that Claire suspected. But if she could find that room and get inside it, maybe she'd discover a clue, something that would link the odd goings-on to one particular person.

She moved like a shadow, piercing the darkness as well as she could with every sense — her eyes, her ears, her intuitive powers. She used her imagination and, trying as much sense memory as she could muster, she shrank from her usual height, 5′ 9″, to a tiny five feet — at least in her mind. She felt as small and light as a kitten as she found her way along the hall toward the staircase that led to the tower. She'd never been near this part of the castle and, for some reason, it frightened her. Still, she had to do it.

She willed her heart to stop its loud thumping and began to climb. The staircase, unlike the newer one that led to the parapet, was rusted and decrepit, and some of the steps were missing. Without looking down, she climbed to the second level, the gaps between the steps seeming to grow larger even as she leaped over them. She was nearly at the top now; she couldn't turn back.

And then, from nowhere, it appeared. Its raucous cry made Claire's blood freeze, an inhuman squawk that mingled rage and terror. She looked up with a gasp, and for a brief second they were frozen, staring at each other. Standing on the level above her was a masked creature wearing a top hat and cape. Its plastic mask had no features, and because it stood so much higher up than Claire, it was impossible for her to tell how tall it was — or in fact, *what* it was — man, woman, or ghost. The only thing she could tell was that it was holding a bundle concealed under the cape.

"Stop!" she yelled.

But it was too late. The creature turned a corner and vanished into thin air. It was almost as if she'd never seen it at all.

Suddenly, the terror of what might have happened overcame her, and she fled, half-running, half-falling down the broken steps. She could have been killed! And yet, what was even more horrifying was how the creature had come and gone, without a trace. She might have imagined the whole thing — which meant that she might be going mad. No one else in the company, except for Kim who was wildly superstitious, seemed to think anything strange was going on. They hadn't heard voices, and as far as they were concerned, the incidents of the scissors in the mannequin and Claire being locked in the trap were "pranks" or "accidents." She was the only one who believed there was evil in the old castle.

Claire stumbled to the bottom of the stairs and collapsed in a heap, soothing her ragged breathing back to a semblance of normal rhythm. Was it true? Had her overtaxed mind snapped? Had she conjured up this vision, dressed like Ben in its top hat and cape, and then made it disappear?

Too tired and frightened to think clearly, Claire found her way back to her room. Mechanically, she threw off her clothes, took a very hot shower, and fell into bed. Kim hadn't come back to the room, and for once, Claire was glad to be alone here. If there was something wrong with her, she didn't want anyone else to know about it. Briefly, she thought about calling her parents and telling them she was quitting and coming home. But just before she fell asleep, she canceled that idea. No reason why a little insanity should prevent her from enjoying her summer job. And if she weren't imagining things? If it was all real? She didn't know which possibility she dreaded more.

The next morning after breakfast, Ed came to pick her up in his jeep. The backseat was crammed with assorted newspapers and a large picnic basket, prepared for them, Ed announced proudly, by Mrs. Beckman.

"But she made me promise to bring you home to meet her afterwards," Ed grinned as they climbed into the car and started off toward Middlefield.

"What? Sorry, I guess I wasn't listening," Claire apologized. She tried to shake the fog from her head, but she simply couldn't. She'd slept deeply, so soundly that the daylight and reality seemed a rude intrusion on her dreams. Had she dreamed the masked stranger, or had he actually been there on the stairs leading to the tower? All she could think of as they drove along the cool, wooded roads was that she had to get into that tower room, even if it cost her her sanity.

"Boy, do *you* look preoccupied." Ed glanced at her as they sped along the road.

"Do I? Sorry."

"You said that already. Stop apologizing and tell me what's eating you."

She looked at him. No, he'd never believe it. "Too much partying and working, I suppose," she fibbed. "It's nice to have a day off."

"You said it. Saturdays are always special to me. And wait'll you see the falls!"

She smiled wanly, thinking how lucky he was

to be living with a nice normal couple like the Beckmans, away from the craziness of Blairmore Castle. He seemed so . . . innocent, yes, that was the word. Whereas what she had been through for the past week could curdle a person's blood. She pulled at her dark curls absently and then grasped her gold heart. She held onto it all the way to Glendale Falls — for luck.

Middlefield was a sleepy town, made up of the short main street and lots of winding dirt roads. There was a general store (which also housed the post office and the town's only gas station), two churches, a town hall, and that was it. They drove past civilization and wound their way down Chipman Road out to the falls.

"Hear them?" Ed asked as he parked in the small, sandy space reserved for just five or six cars.

"I think so."

"In the springtime they're so loud you can't hear yourself think. June's tame compared to April. C'mon." He took the picnic basket in one hand and her arm in the other, and together they walked down a rough-hewn path to the flat rocks where the falls began. They were huge, descending terraces, the clear water sparkling and pouring off one ledge onto another. Ed and Claire hopscotched their way around the ledges, settling on one where they could watch the biggest cascade — a twenty-foot fountain that fell off the sheer cliff and landed in the basin far below them.

"It's wonderful out here," Claire nodded, her fears forgotten for the moment. And it was true that out here in the midst of nature, the illusory world where Claire had literally been closeted for the past nine days seemed unimportant, almost unreal. She was quiet for a long time, holding Ed's hand and listening to the regular flow of the crystal waters. After a while, without speaking, they got up and walked, circling the rocks and climbing down, then looking up toward the source of the falls.

"Feel better?" Ed asked her once.

She smiled, but still didn't speak. It was comforting just to let the mood of the place wash over her, to settle her mind as it cleansed her body.

The day passed much too quickly — their lovely, private picnic; then a quick dip in the cold, clear water; and finally another walk around. By the time they climbed back into Ed's jeep, it was already three-thirty.

"Oh gosh, I've got to get to rehearsal. Do you think Mrs. Beckman will give me a raincheck?" Claire asked in a panic, the responsibilities of her job once again looming large.

Ed looked disappointed, then shrugged. "Sure she will. I'm afraid, though, if I don't bring you around soon, she'll think you're a figment of my wild imagination."

Claire laughed nervously. "Yeah, well . . . what can we do?" Bursting at the seams to let out her suspicions about her own imagination and the hidden room, yet not daring to tell him a thing, Claire sat quietly on the ride back to the theater. As she jumped down from her seat, she had a silly impulse to grab him around the neck and kiss him. Instead, she said, "This was great, really. Thanks, Ed."

She ran down the gravel drive and through the huge, medieval doors, trying to hold the day inside her as she raced down the corridor to the theater. For a change, she was early. Sean and Stephanie were talking down in the first row and Kim and David were working on their final scene together downstage right. Ben, who'd complained that he never really got to see the show because of the cabaret, was sitting on the left aisle. The other actors were milling around, nobody quite sure of what Sean had in mind for today's brush-up rehearsal.

He clapped his hands loudly, drawing everyone's attention. "All right, folks, just wanted to say congratulations on last night. All in all it was" — he paused dramatically — "acceptable."

There was a groan from the assembled troops.

"No, really, there were a lot of good things in the performance. But I'm not going to heap you with praise because I don't want anyone resting on his fat head and goofing off. You've got a show tonight, and then tomorrow we start rehearsals for the next play in the repertory, so I want you on your toes. Now, why don't we run the last act just for variety. Don't work too hard; just go through the motions. That way you won't be stale for tonight. Okay, Act Three, Scene One. Oh, wait a second, Kim, would you take that dive for the gun once or twice before we start? It still looks like you're tripping on your shoe-laces."

"Yes, Simon Legree," Kim smirked. "David, give me the cue, would you?"

David crossed his arms, an odd smile on his face. " 'I'll just stick around until I get what I came for,' " he recited in a strange, faraway voice.

Kim sighed loudly and took the move, skidding forward toward her mark. But as Claire and the others watched, astounded, she kept going, unable to break her fall. With a scream, she toppled forward into the orchestra pit, landing heavily five feet below the stage.

"Oh no!" Claire ran down the aisle, drawn to the scene with a sense of dread. Sean and Stephanie were in the pit, bending over Kim who lay in a crumpled heap, her left leg bent at an odd angle beneath her. Her eyes were closed.

"Her leg's broken. Don't move her. Well, somebody get Doc Geller on the phone!" Sean yelled.

Claire moved as fast as she could, tearing back down the aisle to get to the box office where the nearest phone was located. She passed Ryan at a gallop, but he caught her arm when he saw the look on her face.

"What is it?"

"Kim — she broke her leg. She fell off the stage and passed out."

Ryan shoved the can of 3-in-1 oil he was holding in his back pocket. "Jeez, that's bad. Better call an ambulance."

"Well, let me go and I will," Claire exploded, tearing away from him and running down the hall to the lobby. She leaped at the phone, much to the consternation of the box-office clerk, dialed the operator, and told her to call an ambulance. Then she got Doc Geller's nurse on the phone and explained the situation.

"You tell them to wait for the ambulance. Don't you try to take her anywhere. The doctor'll meet them at the hospital," the nurse instructed.

It was with a heavy heart that Claire walked back into the theater. Everything seemed in total turmoil — Stephanie holding Kim's head, David pacing the aisle, Ben standing anxiously on the apron of the stage, Sean tracing the path Kim had taken before her fall. Just as Claire reached the pit, she saw Sean bend down and rub at something on the stage floor. "What the hell!" he muttered.

"What did you find?" Stephanie asked.

"Oil. There's a patch of something oily right where Kim's mark was. She must have skidded and couldn't stop." He stood up, his face rigid with anger. "How the —?"

Claire blinked, her mind's eye seeing a can of oil. Where had she just seen it? *Oh, but it couldn't be Ryan,* she thought at once. *How absurd! Now you're suspecting everybody.*

And yet, it made sense. Hadn't Ed said that Ryan hated actresses? Could he be responsible for all the weird stuff that had been going on? Of course, Ryan carried that oil can around all the time — he did need it occasionally in his work. And when Ed said he hated actresses, he didn't mean his brother was out to get anybody who "tread the boards," as the saying went.

Claire looked at the faces around her, each

of them clearly concerned about Kim. There was David, his egocentric smirk gone; a white-faced Sean; and capable, caring Stephanie. But any one of them could have done it. Then Ryan walked in with the ambulance attendants and Claire was forced to consider the possibility that the very person she liked best, and the one who appeared to be the kindest, could also be guilty.

What am I doing? she moaned inwardly. *Next thing, I'll be suspecting that I did it because I've lost my mind.*

"I'll go with her, Sean," she heard Stephanie say. "You guys go back to work."

Claire saw them conferring quietly for a moment, and she knew that they were discussing what to do about Kim's part. It was conceivable that Stephanie could do the role if it were re-written slightly, but did they have time for that now? Stephanie didn't even know the lines or the blocking.

"Well, honey, how about it?" Sean's firm hand rested on Claire's shoulder, and she jumped as she realized what he meant.

"I —"

"You know the part perfectly. I bet you could do it in your sleep," he said in a fatherly tone. He wasn't going to beg — he was simply telling her what was what.

"I think I know it, but —" She was so excited she couldn't even think straight. This was the chance every understudy dreamed of, to go on at a moment's notice and steal the show. But Claire couldn't help feeling awful at the same time. If this hadn't happened to Kim, she would never have been asked to act in a main-stage show. And yet, fate — or someone's evil shenanigans — had thrown a plum role right in her lap.

"I know you know it. Let's start at the beginning. Places, please." Then, as an afterthought, he called into the house, "Ladies and gentlemen, due to unforseen circumstances, the part of Peggy Morris, which was to have been played by Kim Dresden, will be performed by Claire Allenton — until further notice."

In a daze, Claire felt herself helped up onstage to a smattering of encouraging applause. Only Ryan, now busy pouring sand on the oil that had caused Kim's accident, didn't look up as Claire took her place. But she was too busy furiously muttering her first-act lines to worry about him.

She called Ed as soon as the run-through was over. "You'll never guess what happened!" she said breathlessly into the receiver.

"Let's see . . . a scandal? Something I can put in the paper?"

"Kim broke her leg and I got her part."

"What? Slow down, for heaven's sake. How'd she break her leg?"

Claire tried to tell the whole story slowly and coherently, but she was too worked up. Her mixed feelings about her good fortune and how she had come by it confused her.

"But, well that's . . . I don't know, Claire. Who put oil on the stage?"

She was silent, not wanting to mention her earlier suspicion. Ed thought she was weird enough already.

"Anyone could have done it. Or I suppose someone could have spilled it there accidentally without noticing. Will you come see me in the show tonight? Please."

This time, he was silent. Then he sighed and said reluctantly, "I wish you weren't involved in this, Claire."

"Involved? What do you mean?"

"I can't come tonight," Ed said brusquely instead of answering her.

She was so hurt, she didn't know how to respond. "Can't — or won't?"

"Claire, don't nag. I said I can't. I have something to do. I'll come tomorrow night, how's that?"

She bit back her angry words and tried not to sound as disappointed as she really was. "Whatever. Okay. I'll see you."

"I won't say break a leg, okay?" he laughed, but she didn't respond to his extremely unfunny joke.

"See you tomorrow," she barked and hung up.

Then she called the hospital to see how Kim was and Stephanie answered. She told Claire that the leg had been neatly broken, in only one place. The doctor said it would heal pretty quickly — in six to eight weeks. "Kim's sleeping now — they gave her something for the pain — but she wishes you luck," Stephanie said before she hung up. "And so do I," she added kindly. "Lots of it, though you don't need it."

Stephanie really sounded as though she meant that, and Claire was instantly guilty for ever having suspected her. The woman was quiet and kept to herself, but she was enormously generous — both with her time and with her comments.

With her mind a little more at ease, Claire began to prepare for the performance. She read through her part again and choked down a little dinner, then bolted down to the dressing room. Maggie had found a suitable costume in the racks that fit her. As Claire sat at Kim's mirror before the half-hour call, she had to admit that she was glad Ed wouldn't be there — she'd be too nervous trying to be good for him to really concentrate on her character. If only he hadn't been so nasty about the whole thing.

There was a knock at the door.

"Yes," she called, her voice suddenly cracking and her stomach filling up with butterflies.

"It's just me." Ryan walked in, a bunch of hastily gathered wild flowers in his hand. "You better be good, Claire," he said in a shy, funny voice, dropping the flowers on the dressing table. He was out the door before she could say thank you.

She picked up the little bouquet and hugged it briefly to her chest. *What a nice gesture,* Claire mused. *Just like him, too. How stupid to have imagined that Ryan could ever harbor a menacing thought toward anyone.*

"Five minutes, Miss Allenton," Bob Lynch called.

"Yikes!" Claire responded and went to take her place for the curtain.

CHAPTER
7

"I wish you'd reconsider, Kim," Claire sighed. She sat forlornly at the foot of Kim's bed, slowly, helping her roommate pack.

"But what am I going to do here?" Kim asked frankly. "I can't earn my salary acting, and you know I'm all thumbs at a sewing machine, even if Maggie'd have me. No, I think I'll go back to my little hovel in Manhattan and read plays while I heal. The Workman's Comp. will keep me in tuna fish."

"You could take a summer vacation here and read all you want," Claire protested. She didn't want to admit that she was terribly anxious about being left alone here. And since the night in the dressing room when Kim had yelled at her for whistling, they hadn't talked about their fears.

"I could do that," Kim nodded, setting her heavy sweater on top of her other clothing and pushing down the suitcase lid. "But then I'd have to watch you doing a fabulous job in the play and rehearsing for the next one and sitting through the same show every night. At least in New York I can get someone to take me to the movies." Kim grinned and patted Claire's hand. "You can do it on your own, kid. You really are terrific in the part."

Claire blushed and pretended bashfulness, scuffing her feet on the flagstone floor. "Aw shucks, Ma'am. T'weren't nothin'." Then she looked intently into Kim's face. "You're not just saying that? You really think so?"

"Don't fish for compliments, girl! You already got the highest accolade the Becket Bugle can award, and your boyfriend didn't even write the review."

"Ed is *not* my —"

"The audiences love you, the critic thought you were 'funny, sad, and striking,' and what more do you want? By the way, I hear Sean's thinking of a nice juicy role for you in the Neil Simon comedy they're doing in August."

"Who told you?" Claire's eyes were shining. Her very first professional role, and she was a success. Her parents, of course, had been incredulous when she phoned to tell them, and were anxiously awaiting Mr. Allenton's vacation in July when they could fly up and see her. But Claire didn't need to show off in front of them — she could feel in her bones that she was doing well. Only one week in the part and already she'd made it her own. The other nice thing was that Ed had made a huge fuss over her — something that must have been hard for him to do, given his feelings about the theater.

"Who told me? A little bird, natch," Kim

winked. "He also said there are great things in store for you. Well, I guess I'm ready. Want to carry my bags, baby?"

"If you insist." Claire picked up the suitcases as Kim hobbled to the door on her crutches. Then Kim turned and looked back at the room. "Guard this girl and keep her free from harm," she told the old walls. She gave a silly little salute and walked out.

Claire shivered as she walked after her down the long corridor. She had heard that woman's voice through the wall every night now, although she hadn't mentioned it to anyone. Nor had she breathed a word about the masked creature — if she didn't talk about it, she reasoned, she might just forget it. Kim seemed to sleep so soundly these nights, and how she could do it with that eerie, high-pitched screaming going on was unfathomable to Claire. Unless, of course, she really had cracked and this was all in her mind.

She had a feeling now, an intimation, that something else would happen. Something — or someone — was waiting to strike again, waiting for everyone's guard to be down before continuing with the horrible pranks. Every once in a while, standing in the wings waiting to go on, or working in the shop, Claire would find that she was holding her breath, watching and waiting. She would have to stop herself from examining all of them — Sean, Stephanie, David, Bob, Ryan, even Ben —looking for a motive, a reason. And then, stumped, she'd go back to work.

The two girls reached the front hall, where the cast and crew had assembled to say their goodbyes. Everyone had a kiss and a few words for Kim, and there were tears in her eyes when she finally tore herself away and walked over to David, who was driving her to the bus stop. "Oh, you're all so great," she sighed. "I'll come up and see a show at the end of the season, okay?" Then she hugged everyone a second time and David propelled her gently out the door.

Claire watched the car disappear down the drive, thinking how comforting it had been to have a roommate, someone to share things with, no matter how awful they might be. And now that she was going to be alone, well . . .

She found herself clutching her gold heart as she walked back into the depths of the castle and wound her way down the stairs to the shop. *I will not pick up Kim's superstitious nature*, she vowed as she went to work on a bookcase she was painting for the second show, which was now in rehearsal. She would try to keep herself sane and calm, for as long as she could.

But as the day progressed, Claire found herself obsessed with that hidden room and the voices she heard coming from it. As soon as the performance ended that evening, and she had quickly changed out of her costume and makeup, she returned to her room. She couldn't just sit back and wait for things to happen! It seemed vitally important now, with Kim gone, that she discover what was going on before something else occurred. She tried to read by the light of her flashlight, but her mind just wasn't on anything except her mission.

It must have been past midnight when that

high, filtered laugh floated down through the walls. Claire jumped and sat up in bed, nervously shining the flashlight into every corner, as if she feared that the voice had crept in under the locked door.

Naturally, she saw nothing. She flicked off the light and sat for a brief moment, mustering her courage. Then she stuck the flashlight in the back pocket of her jeans and valiantly walked across the room. She unlocked the door and stared into the dark corridor.

"You're a fool," she whispered to herself as she struck out for the stairs that led to the tower. Tonight she'd do it. Tonight, she was going to find the hidden room.

Looking only straight ahead of her, she proceeded down the hall, trying not to imagine what might happen to her if she encountered whoever —or whatever — had been out to get her and then Kim. It was unusual, she thought as she started to climb the rickety stairs, but nobody else in the company, as far as she knew, had heard or seen anything that would lead them to believe in either ghosts or murderers.

She was at the first landing now, exactly where she'd seen the masked figure. She stopped to catch her breath and look around, but all was silent. As she proceeded upward, she heard a choked sob. Then, the silvery voice spoke. What was it? Claire distinctly heard a woman's voice. "It's only games," came the hollow words.

"Into the flames," responded a man's voice.

This is insane, Claire thought. *I should go right back and tell somebody and get them to come with me.* But the voices might be gone by then, she thought in a panic.

As she reached the next landing, the stairs seemed to drop off into space. There was a huge gap, too big for her to leap, up to the last set of steps that must have led directly to the tower. She hung suspended in space, wondering where in the world that masked creature could have disappeared to.

"Unless he's a ghost and can walk through walls," she whispered to herself, leaning her weight to balance herself on the wall that these few steps clung to like moss. She stumbled and nearly fell into space, catching herself just in time. The wall had moved!

She pushed frantically and the whole side of stone turned inward. As she flashed her light inside, she gasped with astonishment. The fake wall opened into an old library, the cobwebs heavy on the dusty books.

I found it! she thought excitedly, not daring to make a sound as she jumped over the banister to get inside the hidden room.

Moving stealthily, she took a few steps forward. Then she halted, puzzled by the silence. Clearly, she'd found what she was looking for, and yet there was no one in sight. As a matter of fact, the room looked as though no one had been inside it for years — the dust was spread out like a white veil over the huge green velvet Victorian sofa and armchair; the cobwebs obscured the titles of the leather-bound books; the Oriental carpet was worn and threadbare.

"But I know the voices came from here," Claire

said aloud, perturbed to have risked life and limb only to find an empty library. How could the people — assuming there *had been* people in here and Claire wasn't out of her mind and hearing things — how could they have gotten out?

"Phooey," she stated, not wanting to admit to herself that she was in fact thrilled not to have found anyone. What would they have done to her if she'd discovered them here?

"Well, maybe I'll find something good to read," she said with false bravery. Pushing aside the cobwebs, she flashed her light on some of the titles. There was Dickens and the complete Jane Austen, also a lot of Thackeray and Byron. Claire was fascinated as she took each old volume off the shelf and flipped through the yellowed pages. There had to be a lot of first editions here — they were really valuable. Wouldn't Ed be excited when she brought him up here!

Half an hour passed quickly as she examined the room and its contents. It was a real treasure trove to an antique lover — she kept imagining her mother oohing and ahing over the exquisite furniture and knickknacks. Claire had completely forgotten the time and what she'd come looking for when her hand touched a book on one of the shelves that somehow didn't feel like a book. And it didn't come off the shelf when she pulled at it, either. The one next to it was identical. Her flashlight revealed that they were made of wood and fixed to the shelf.

"What the — ?" Her hand scanned the false books carefully, investigating them with mixed fear and curiosity. On the left side of the second book was a brass latch; on the right side of the first one was an open chink.

Claire shone the flashlight above her head and peered through. She was able to make out another room on the other side of the bookcase, a room with no visible means of entry. *This* was the hidden room — this was the place where those voices emanated from.

As Claire's eyes became accustomed to the dark, she began to make out shapes. There was a canopied bed in one corner, an elaborate dressing table and armoire in another. Her eyes came to rest on an Empire chaise lounge, and then she started back away from the chink, amazed by what she'd seen. How could it be possible!

Daring to look through again, she confirmed the vision. There was a small woman lying on that chaise, perfectly still, sound asleep. Her long hair lay curling and lustrous on her creamy shoulders, and her gown fit her delicate figure as though it had been custom-made for her. This had to be the women whose voice she kept hearing, Claire thought as she watched her. But where was the man?

As she examined the woman more closely, she noticed something strange about her. She was so waxen, almost lifeless in sleep. She didn't appear to be breathing — her chest didn't move at all.

Who was she? She was so tiny, practically child-size. There was something so odd, so fragile about her. Claire suddenly thought of the day they'd found the dressmaker's dummy, wearing Kim's costume, impaled with a pair of scissors.

There was a tiny dress, cut to ribbons, on Kim's hanger, she recalled. A child's dress? Or a dress designed for a woman just the size of the one who lay on the chaise, still as death.

Claire broke out in an icy sweat as she stood there, glued to the chink. The hairs on the back of her neck raised like those of a frightened kitten as she understood, finally, what she was seeing. The woman beyond the bookcase was dead. Something — or someone — had killed her.

Claire jerked away from the hole as though it had burned her eyes. Her hands were shaking and she had to steady herself by clutching the two wooden books. Who could have done this, and why? Did this woman have something to do with Kim's accident? Or was it that Kim, with all her strange superstitions, had stumbled on the truth and had found out about this hidden room? It was fairly easy to deduce that whoever had killed this woman had also caused Kim to slip and fall onstage and had caused Claire to be locked in the trap overnight. Naturally, the high, silvery voice she and Kim had heard through the wall was that of this poor woman, who would never speak again. How she got into the theater without anyone knowing about it, was what Claire couldn't figure out.

Forcing herself to lean forward, Claire once again put her eyes to the chink to look at the horrible sight. She'd have to tell Sean, of course, and once she'd told Ed, it would be in the paper. There'd be an investigation and probably they'd close down the theater. And Claire would go home to Maryland and continue her nice, normal existence, the one she'd known before she came to Blairmore Castle.

Unless the killer decided to get rid of her, too.

She shuddered, studying the tiny figure on the chaise. She was so lovely, with that profusion of curls surrounding her calm face. It was too dark to see what color her hair or dress was, but the gown she wore was really elegant — old-fashioned and flowing, like a Grecian robe, but low-cut, revealing her shoulders and neck. She was so perfect, almost like a doll.

Almost like a mannequin, Claire thought suddenly. Yes, of course, that was it! She was made of wood — that's why she was so still. Not dead — she'd never been alive.

Claire felt tears of relief spring to her eyes, and she greedily searched the length of the figure for other clues. The hands were stiff — they didn't fold down on one another. The feet lay at odd angles, just the way Howard's and Boko's did when Ben wasn't working them.

Ben. The last of Claire's suspects, and the one she had most hoped to be wrong about. But it did make sense. A man who'd lost two wives and his eyesight in this very theater, a person who had to be incredibly angry at the world, however mild-mannered he seemed. And now that Claire thought about it, she remembered how perfectly he managed to walk around and perform ordinary tasks without any assistance. How dashing he'd looked at the cabaret in his top hat and cape, and how, with just a mask covering his face, he could have worn that same costume up here to the hidden room to do . . .

To do what? Why was he keeping this dummy up here, hidden away? And what did she have to do with his vendetta against her and Kim? And what might he do next?

Claire got a grip on herself, took one more look at the lovely mannequin, and slowly found her way out of the old library, carefully drawing back the fake wall as she jumped clear, onto the steps.

The worst of it, she thought, would be telling Ryan and Ed. They wouldn't believe her at first, of course, and she'd probably lose the nicest relationship she'd ever had with a boy in the process of exposing his father. But it had to be done. Before something really terrible happened.

CHAPTER
8

"I think you two have done a terrific job on
the light plot for Stephanie's show," Sean
told Ryan and Claire the next morning. He per-
sisted in calling this second play, "Stephanie's
show" which pleased his wife and annoyed
David, who really had the starring role.

"I need a lot of hardware I don't have, though,"
Ryan said. "You mind if I go into town and
spend a couple of bucks?"

"No, go on. You go with him, Claire. You look
lousy, if you don't mind my saying so. I think
you've been working too hard. Go ahead, the
fresh air'll put a few roses back in your cheeks."
He gave her a fatherly pat on the back and she
smiled half-heartedly. It was difficult to have a
secret like this, but she felt she owed it to Ryan
and Ed to tell them first. But Claire had never
been a whiz at keeping secrets. She didn't know
how to act normal, and when she'd seen Ben at
breakfast this morning, she'd practically bolted
out of the room. It wasn't as easy as it seemed.
First of all, Ben would be the last person anyone

would suspect of anything. Second, nothing had actually happened yet that would let her point a finger. All the odd occurrences *could* have been accidents.

"Okay, thanks, Sean. I'd like to go out for a while." She smiled wanly.

"We'll be back by lunch," Ryan promised.

They drove to Becket through a steady downpour, neither of them talking much. Claire wondered what Ryan really knew about his father, about that third mannequin of his. If only she could think of a decent way to broach the subject.

"You've been in theater ever since you were a kid, Ed told me," she said when they reached the outskirts of town.

"All my life," he nodded. "It's an addiction — what can I do?"

"In your blood, I guess," she said, leading him on.

"What do you mean?" He glanced over at her, an unsettled look in his gray eyes. "Oh, you mean my father."

"Right. And your mother and stepmother."

"I don't remember anything about my mother," he said curtly, "and not a whole lot about my stepmother." He pulled into an open space and parked. "Hardware store's over there," he pointed. "You can go wander. I'll meet you in the coffee shop in twenty."

"Sure," she sighed. *Well, that was a bust,* she thought as she walked across the street. She passed the Becket Bugle office and turned the corner, her goal Joe's Diner where they all hung out when they went into town for anything. She

105

was not exactly surprised to see Ed sitting in a corner booth going over some tearsheets.

"Good morning!" He smiled as Claire approached. "Sorry I haven't been around in a while," he added. "Things have been completely hectic here."

"It's okay. I've been too pooped after performances to sit up and look at the stars, anyway." This wasn't exactly true, and she was disappointed that he'd stayed away so long. She wondered if it was because of her or something else.

"I'm supposed to be at my desk writing a story, but it's a madhouse in there. I can't hear myself think. So I walked over here," he explained, giving her that wonderful intent look that never failed to make her feel warm all over.

"I came into town with Ryan for supplies," she said quickly. "He'll be here in a few minutes," she added as the waitress came over to take her order. She asked for two coffees, one for her and one for Ryan, and settled back in the booth. Once again, she noticed the lovely light blue color of Ed's eyes, and she kicked herself under the table for caring so much about whether or not he was really interested in her.

Claire noticed that he didn't seem overly thrilled at the prospect of having a cup of coffee with his brother.

"It won't kill you," she said.

"I never said —"

"Ed, forget that. I don't really care about that now. I've discovered something. I know you think I'm crazy and overly dramatic, but I really think I know who's behind all the weird stuff that's been going on."

"Good. Who?" he asked skeptically.

"I can't tell you that yet. First I want to show you something at the theater."

"Do you really believe — ?"

They were interrupted as Ryan walked into the diner. Claire waved him over to the table, and the brothers said a cool hello.

"I was just telling Ed," Claire said pointedly, "that there's something you two should know about." She'd thought long and hard about how to do this. It was only fair to let Ed and Ryan in on it first before telling everybody. Anyway, there was still a slim possibility that she could be wrong.

"What's that? More voices in the walls?" Ryan asked.

She didn't remember mentioning that to him. Kim must have told him in one of her superstitious fits.

"It's about that, yes. I wanted to see where the voices were coming from, and last night I found out."

"Well, don't keep us in suspense," Ed laughed.

"There's a hidden room in the castle, just off the top landing that leads to the tower. You push against the wall and it opens into a library."

"Claire, have you gotten enough sleep lately?" Ed gave her a disbelieving look. Ryan was silent.

"Don't you dare make fun of me, Ed Clark. That's not all. On the other side of one of the bookcases is a dressing room. I can't figure out how you get in, but you can see it through a chink between the books."

Ed gave Ryan a look. "Did you know about this?"

But Claire didn't give him time to answer. "I saw something very interesting in the dressing room. There's a female mannequin all dressed up, lying on a chaise longue."

"Oh? What do you make of that?" Ed was suddenly curious.

"I guess it's one of Ben's." She looked at Ryan for confirmation. He licked his lips, as if debating with himself how much to say.

"I did see a female dummy years ago when I was a kid. Ben used to work on her constantly, perfecting her voice, commissioning costumes for her. But you know Dad," he said to his brother. "Such a perfectionist. He didn't think she was good enough for the act, and he couldn't figure out how to work her in with Howard and Boko."

"I never knew he had a girl dummy," Ed commented.

"He hardly ever talked about her, even to me. I kind of thought he'd given up on her. Guess not." Ryan turned to Claire with a pleading look on his face. "Don't tell anybody about her, okay, Claire? Or about that room you found. She's kind of a testament to his own failure, something he wanted so badly but could never have. The way I read it, she's not a dummy — she's an obsession."

Claire started when she heard the word. "Maybe . . . maybe somebody should talk to

Ben. Maybe you both should." She wouldn't be the one to imply that there was anything serious to worry about. She wanted the brothers to come to this conclusion on their own.

They were silent, staring at the table. Ed seemed at a loss, as if he'd just gone through the final separation from the father he'd scarcely known at all.

"I think," he said at last, "if he wants a private place to work on another character for his act, that's his business." Ed frowned and shook his head. "Claire, you told me yourself that people in theater get hooked on stuff that the rest of us — I mean, people like me," he corrected himself, putting Claire and Ryan in the other camp, "don't get involved in."

"But those voices in the wall," Claire protested.

"So?"

"I never told you, but I saw him one night on the staircase, wearing a mask. It was —"

"Maybe he was getting ready for Halloween," Ed snapped, getting up from the table and throwing a couple of dollars down. "Who cares what he was doing? I'm going back to work." Disgustedly, he stormed out of the diner, leaving Claire and Ryan sitting nervously together.

After a long pause, Claire asked, "What do *you* think?"

"Okay. He's — Ben's not crazy or anything," he said slowly.

"I never said he was. But don't you think . . ." she said hesitantly, ". . . isn't it possible . . ."

"I wish you'd cool it with the detective stuff, Claire. You really don't know anything about my family." He got up, his quirky, friendly face set in serious concern.

She was immediately embarrassed, because of course, he was right. "I'm sorry. I was only trying to help."

"Yeah, sure. Let's get back. Sean'll be wondering."

"Ryan." She put a hand on his, but he drew away, clearly annoyed by her persistence. "Just tell me one thing. Ben *was* blinded in the fire that destroyed Blairmore, wasn't he?"

"What?" He turned to her sharply. "Who told you that?"

"Nobody. I just figured that since he'd been lighting director before, it was probably — "

"Well, you're wrong. He was in a car crash. Anything else you want to know?"

"No." She got up and walked around the side of the table. "I guess I do have a pretty vivid imagination. It's just that I'm worried about him, is all. I really like your father, Ryan."

"Sure." He paid for their coffees and left the diner in silence, warning Claire that perhaps she had gone too far. What right did she, a stranger, have to conjecture about other people's parents?

She followed him out of the diner, a picture forming in her mind of that awful crash, a car bursting into flames, Ben at the wheel covering his eyes and then —

She didn't want to think about it anymore; she didn't want to think of the angry, distorted visions that now lay behind that man's sightless eyes. But hard as she tried, she couldn't stop thinking.

That night at dinner, she found it difficult to keep up a cheery front. She didn't want anyone to notice her mood, so she sat, pretending to be immersed in the script of a new play.

"So I says to him, really, you got a lot of nerve trying to sell me that heap and call it a car," Bob Lynch guffawed to Ryan. "The man actually thought I was born yesterday."

"Well, weren't you?" Sean quipped from the other side of the table.

"He was, believe me, he was," Ryan chimed in.

"No, dears," Stephanie laughed, her dark voice rising above the others, "*I* am the one who was born yesterday."

Everyone within earshot laughed, except Claire. Stephanie, gorgeous as she was, had a thing about revealing her true age.

"Mrs. McLeod," Ben said when the laughter had died down. "I would like to compliment you on this excellent meal. Truly a culinary masterpiece."

Claire looked up in time to see Mrs. McLeod blush and stammer her thanks.

"I am in agreement," the hollow voice of Howard piped up. He was seated on Ben's knee. "However, I do object to the beverage. Who ever heard of serving milk with roast quail? I should dearly like a glass of champagne."

"I'll take a Coke." Boko's squeaky sound made everyone smile, except Claire. "And that's no quail, my friend. You can wail, but you won't get quail. All you'll get is chicken!" He made a lip-smacking noise. "And that's what you got!"

Although everyone appeared to be enjoying the dummies' tiff, just the sound of them set Claire off again. She got up from the table, folding her script under her arm.

"You leaving, Claire?" Stephanie asked.

"I've — I want to look over a few things before the show," she muttered, rushing from the dining room. Until she had proof positive that Ben was dangerous and responsible for all the "accidents," she should be *acting* the part of his friend. Instead, she was behaving like a class-A victim in a horror story. The one the killer always gets because she's too terrified to take logical steps to protect herself.

She paced the parapet for the next hour, and then slowly made her way downstairs to get ready for the show. At least the performance would take her mind off her fears. There was nothing as therapeutic as losing herself in a character.

She dressed in her costume, then draped the makeup towel over her neck and shoulders as she listened to the guys on the other side of the dressing room wall discussing Bob's car problems. She peeled back the paper on her stick of greasepaint and thoughtfully brought it to her face.

"You better watch it, girl," she whispered to her reflection. "Keep on like this and your hair will turn white overnight. You'll never play an ingenue again."

She grinned at her own joke and started on her makeup. At the ten-minute call, she got up and stretched as she always did before a show, bending to each side and doing a quiet vocal warmup, just as her drama coach had taught her. As she leaned over to touch her toes, her gold heart fell to the floor in front of her.

"Oh, no," she wailed. As she picked it up, she noticed that the clasp had come loose, probably because she was always pulling on it for luck.

"Places, please!" Bob called.

She hated to go onstage without it, but what could she do? "I'm not going to turn superstitious like Kim," she vowed. "I can give a perfectly good performance without it. And tomorrow, Ryan can drive me into Becket to the jeweler's." She looked at it longingly, then placed it on the dressing table. Swiftly and surely, she mounted the steps to the backstage area.

The audience was hushed now — she could hear the rustle of programs and gentle coughs and murmurs. Peeking through the hole, she spotted Ed sitting in one of the actors' reserved seats. The sight of him made her glad and made the incidents that had come before insignificant, at least temporarily. She would give, not a good performance tonight, but a great one.

Act One went smoothly, her monologue got a small round of applause, and David restrained himself from stealing their scene. As the curtain came down and Claire rushed downstairs to change into her next costume, she felt a new confidence about her acting. It was strange how all these weird goings-on had strengthened her in a way. If she could take Ben's nasty tricks and come out on top, she could probably do anything.

By the time Act Two got underway, she felt

like she was flying, and was only sorry that she had to get killed off so soon because she, and the audience, were having so much fun. She approached her death scene a little differently tonight, and David responded beautifully. He thrived on improvisation.

In the scene, she was supposed to be hanging a picture and telling David's character about her suspicions. As she talks, her back turned to David, she goes on blithely working as he stalks her with the breakaway chair. The audience can see what's going to happen to her and is breathless with anticipation.

Tonight, Claire played only half the scene with her back to David, so he had to be much more stealthy about dragging the chair across the stage. They approached the big moment like a cat and mouse in a standoff, each trying to get the better of the other.

"'If your wife got stuck in this snowstorm, the only place she could have gone would have been Gerry Turner's. And he hasn't been right in the head for a year now,'" Claire read.

"'I wouldn't worry about my wife if I were you,'" David said, smiling meanly. He raised the balsa-wood chair swiftly and Claire reminded herself not to flinch. It never came down as hard as she imagined and it always splintered.

The chair hit its mark, just as it always did. And Claire toppled to one side, just as she always did. Except tonight, the chair remained in one piece, and Claire was knocked out cold.

The curtain fell.

CHAPTER
9

Dᴀᴠɪᴅ and Ryan dragged her offstage and Sean ran to get a cold compress for her head.

"I don't understand," David muttered. "Claire checks props herself before she gets into make-up. Good thing I only hit her with the side of it."

"She's coming around. Claire . . ." Sean spoke in soothing tones. "Claire, honey, wake up, sweetheart."

Groggily, she opened her eyes, then let them flutter shut. The right side of her head pounded. "Where's . . . who's . . . ?" she muttered.

She was still half out of it when Ed came running toward them, having seen from his seat in the house that Claire wasn't acting when she was hit.

"I've got the car near the door. I'll take her to the hospital," he said breathlessly.

"No . . . no hospital. . . . Curtain call. . . ." Claire reminded them from her fog.

Sean and David had to laugh. "What a trouper!" Sean quipped. "Or are you just vain? Listen, miss, you're going to the hospital and get that gash in your head fixed. It clashes with your costume, darling."

She sighed and tried to pick up her head, but found it impossible. As she touched it gingerly, her hand came away warm and sticky. She was bleeding.

"Let's get her into the car," Ed insisted. "Ryan, get that two-by-four and help me lift her. Let's not jar her head."

Ryan looked white and shaken as he helped his brother roll Claire onto the board. Together they carried her into the clear night and settled her gently across the backseat of Ed's car.

"I'll phone with a progress report from the hospital," he promised as they drove off.

"Where we going?" Claire muttered, still unable to form full sentences in her mouth. Her brain knew exactly what she wanted to say, but her lips wouldn't make the words.

"I am whisking you away for a romantic evening ride, my dear," Ed told her, trying to sound both silly and seductive. But he was too worried to be convincing.

"It's Ben. Gotta tell you," she blurted out, not really aware of how this was coming out. "Voices, trapdoor, Kim's leg — all of it."

"Sure," Ed said. "You lie still."

"It's Ben," she moaned again. "He switched chairs."

Ed grunted, tolerating this only because he figured she was punchy.

"You don't believe," she sighed. " 'Cause he's your father. Love *my* father, too."

"Claire, you don't know what you're saying," Ed told her firmly.

"You and Ryan were both kids when he got blind in the car crash. So sad," she went on, more to herself than to him. "Where were you when it happened?"

"Car crash? No, Claire. You're confused because you're driving in a car now — but that's not how Ben lost his sight."

"No? Thought it was . . . then how? I have to know."

"It was the fire that destroyed Blairmore Castle. I thought he'd told you that. He was trying to save Adrienne and rushed back in for her, but it was too late."

"Adrienne?"

"My mother," he said shortly. "Her name was Adrienne Auvergne. I was six months old when she died."

"Adrienne," Claire muttered. "Ryan told me it was a car crash, though."

"Yeah, I know. Well, Ryan doesn't like to talk about it — or about her. You know how it is. He was only eight and he'd already lost one mother. Now go to sleep, will you?"

"Um. Okay. It's Ben," she repeated. Groggy as she was, *now* she was sure of it. Ben, who was always able to walk into a room, quietly and carefully, and know just where the furniture was. Ben, who could dress Howard and Boko and be aware of which costume was which. He seemed to have a sixth sense now that he had lost one of the others. And he had every reason to hold a grudge against theater people —

117

sighted actors and crew who lived the life he could only remember.

And yet, how could she possibly convince Ed and Ryan of this, let alone Sean? It seemed hopeless. She lay in the backseat, waiting for the fog to clear, wanting to tell Ed to drive straight to the police and yet knowing she had no way to prove Ben was guilty. She would be branded as an overly dramatic girl who, thanks to the bump on her head, had finally gone off her rocker.

She allowed Ed to fuss over her, and let her arms drape casually around him as he carried her into the emergency room of Pittsfield General Hospital. It felt so nice in his arms, so warm and comfortable, that she could almost forget the blinding pain in her head. Then she let the doctors and nurses take over as she sat down heavily on one of the waiting room wheelchairs.

"It's not concussion," she assured Ed as the hospital paramedics wheeled her off for an examination. "Go home and get some rest." The last thing she saw as they took her through the swinging doors was Ed's sad face, looking longingly after her.

She was put through a battery of tests and found normal, or so she assumed from the vague answers she got to her questions. "If I'm okay," she said to a bored-looking resident some two hours later, "can I go home?"

"Gotta stay overnight for observation," he muttered. "Never know what'll turn up by morning. Could get serious."

As if her head would suddenly overreact and

grow another few ears or foreheads! She tried to protest, but he was gone before she could get a word out.

"In the morning," she said to the antiseptic room. Then she fell asleep.

She was examined again at six, and then at eight. When she demanded to be checked out, she was told she was a minor and would have to wait for her next of kin.

"But I don't have . . . oh, please, doctor," she begged a new resident, a young woman with huge glasses and stringy hair. "I'm an apprentice at the theater in Becket. I have to get back."

"Well, you can call them. If someone responsible picks you up, I'll release you. But you better take it easy for a while, young lady."

"I promise. Now will you let me call?"

The resident shrugged and handed her the receiver. Claire dialed Sean's private number and Stephanie answered.

"Hi! It's me."

"Claire, how *are* you? We called earlier but they wouldn't give us any information," Stephanie said in a breathless tone.

"Well, they're like that over here. Not terribly helpful. But I'm okay and I want to come home. Can you send someone to pick me up?"

"You wait right there. Sean or I will be there in an hour."

As she dressed and signed the checkout form, Claire plotted her next strategy. She would have to be careful. Ben clearly felt threatened now, and she appeared to be the target of his anger.

What about the hidden room? Did he know she'd found it and discovered the female dummy?

She was still pondering all this when the phone rang, jerking her out of her reverie.

"Claire! God, I've been tearing my hair over you!" Ed's voice was a healing balm across the phone wires. "I waited until they kicked me out at 3 A.M. And this morning —"

"I know. I've already called Stephanie and they're picking me up. Thanks for bringing me last night," she added, thinking of the cozy feeling she'd had in his arms.

"Are you sure you're well enough to get out? Maybe a few days in the hospital. . . . You sounded pretty bleary last night, babbling on about some really weird stuff."

"Yeah, I know." She forced an embarrassed laugh. "But you've got to take me as I am, Ed — just a babbling idiot sometimes. Oh, listen, they've come back for me with the stupid wheelchair again. I've got to go. I'll give you a call tonight."

If I'm still able to, she thought grimly, watching the company car pull up to the hospital driveway. Ryan was at the wheel. The sad truth was, Claire was on her own from here on in, and only through a match of wits would she be able to prove to everyone exactly what was going on.

The attendant brought her to the car and Ryan opened the door on the passenger side for her. She climbed in, then smiled at him. "Yes, ladies and gentlemen, she walks, she talks, she survives."

"Pretty amazing," he murmured. "That was quite a clobbering you took last night."

"But what you *don't* know," she said, making light of it on purpose, "is that I have a steel plate in my head that deflected the blow. And also, of course, I have my good luck charm, so I'm completely protected from all harm." She reached up to touch the gold heart, but her fingers closed around air. "Oh, no, I forgot." She shook her head. "I left it on my dressing room table. The clasp broke."

"Guess you better get it fixed," he nodded. "I think you need as much protection as you can get."

They drove back to the theater, both of them quiet, both lost in thought. One thing Claire knew now was that she couldn't depend on the two brothers to believe anything she came up with about their father. And maybe it was only fair that she leave them out of this until the very last moment.

When they arrived back at the theater, Sean was waiting in the driveway, pacing the gravel walk. He opened the car door for her, his brow furrowed with concern. "To bed, young lady," he ordered. "I don't want to see your face for the next three days. We've already rearranged the schedule so your show is off until you're well."

"But I'm perfectly fine," Claire began. Sean's response was to place both hands on her shoulders and steer her in the direction of the castle's front door.

"Not another word," he barked, walking her

briskly down the flagstone halls toward the actors' sleeping quarters.

"Just let me go down to the dressing room a second. I left something important on the table."

"Later," he said. "It can wait."

They were at the door to her room, and he opened it for her. "Claire," he said softly, his usually brusque tone mellowing considerably, "I'm concerned about you. All these accidents — and I know your folks would kill me if they knew the rotten care we've taken of you so far. You, ah . . . you haven't told your father about this yet, have you?"

She looked at him curiously. Why had he asked that? Did he suspect that those "accidents" had a cause?

"No. In all our phone calls I've just raved about the theater and my job. I didn't want to worry them."

"Good girl," Sean sighed, noticeably relieved. "Let's keep it that way, shall we? Particularly since I know nothing else of this . . . ah, strange nature is going to occur again. Get some sleep, sweetheart. We'll see you at dinner."

Claire nestled softly among the pillows, watching the door close after him. There was something in his words that made her uneasy, something that let her know without question that she was not mad, nor had she ever been. Someone was responsible for the "accidents."

Sean knew enough to warn her to keep quiet, but how much else did he know? She spun over the past events in her mind and pondered their various connections. Sean had opened the theater for Alan Craig five years ago; Craig had persuaded him to take Ben on. "Returning to the scene of the crime," Ed had said. Could Craig have told Sean all about Ben's past but insisted he hire him anyway? And why?

Claire wished she could think straighter, wished she had some time to put two and two together. But it would be ridiculous for her to lie here thinking while everyone else was at work. This was her chance!

She took her flashlight, then crept quietly to the door of her room. Not a sound; she was safe. Slipping out, she locked the door behind her and sped down the corridor to the staircase.

Today she leaped up two steps at a time and, when she got to the landing she leaned heavily against the fake wall, which opened with barely a creak. Again, she listened, but she heard nothing except the sound of her own terrified heart. She stepped inside the old library and breathed in the musty air. Then, hardly thinking of her own dread, hardly thinking at all, she closed the door behind her.

The room was surprisingly cozy, the kind of place you'd find in an old country inn, with some old country squire seated at the desk with his pipe, a glass of port, and a good book he'd just taken from the shelf. There was a fireplace, and Claire could imagine a cat curled up before it as snow fell in front of the windows. Except there were no windows in this particular library. The place was shut up like a tomb, and just as quiet.

She shone her light around until it fell on a

standing lamp, a tall brass thing with funny yellow ball fringe around the shade. She turned up the gas, and the room was suddenly illuminated with a hazy yellow light. She could see the stuffed divan, the two heavy leather club chairs, and, of course, the bookcases.

The object of her quest, though, was more illusive. How could she get into the room on the other side? Retracing her steps from the other night, Claire fumbled with the dusty books until she found the two wooden ones. She peered between the chinks, but the room was dark, and she couldn't make out anything inside.

"I know it's all going to make sense if I can get in there and see that dummy again," she whispered, clutching the latch on the left false book. The latch!

She examined it closely, pulling at it to make it give. In her feeble attempt to move the thing, she broke the nail on her index finger right across the cuticle line and she swore with the sudden pain. "Come on, you, move!" she exhorted the latch.

And then it did, sliding imperceptibly to the left. With it went the entire bookcase, shifting like a huge piece of scenery worked by a dozen invisible hands. Creaking and protesting, it finally reached its destination, the opposite wall of the internal chamber, now dimly lit by the glow of the library lamp.

Claire ran inside and lit the small glass lamp on the night table. Then she looked around. The mannequin was no longer on the divan. Claire blinked at the sight that brought a cold sweat to her upper lip and forehead. It was worse than anything she could have imagined, and proof that a very sick mind was at work.

The beautiful doll, dressed in another elegant gown, was bound and gagged, tied to a straight-backed chair in the corner of the room, beside the armoire. Her tiny eyes seemed to plead with Claire, begging to be released. The last thing Claire wanted to do was to touch that dummy, the object of a very peculiar obsession. Despite the fact that she was visibly shaking, she walked toward the imprisoned doll, squinting at her in the light.

The face was perfectly painted, the eyelashes long and curling over clear hazel eyes. The hair looked real and soft — it fell in folds of reddish-brown satin over the milk-white shoulders. To-day's gown was off-white silk, a long sheath with a jeweled belt at the waist. And the little arms, twisted behind the chair, looked so bizarre, as if there were real muscles and tendons being wrenched around in this awful position. Claire shuddered, unable to take her eyes off the creature.

Why was she tied up? What kind of mind would think of something so perverse? What could it mean? She ran through the possibilities, but none of them made sense to her. Ben kept this dummy here to remind him of the past — but *what* about the past? And did Sean know?

She walked over to the dressing table, which was piled high with scrapbooks and empty picture frames. What was really going on, Claire wondered. She flipped open the heavy leather brass binder of the first scrapbook and stared at the cover page. In scrolled black letters, the words "Blairmore Castle, 1958" leaped up at her. She turned the first thick parchment page and began to read. It was an old review of a melodrama that had been performed at Blairmore in Scotland in 1958.

There are few things as fine as an evening of entertainment such as we enjoyed last Saturday eve. The rendition of Thompson's *Old Peaked Hat* was the sort of theatre we haven't seen this side of Aberdeen since the days of McGiven and Kneeland. As Patsy, Adrienne Auvergne was sheer perfection — a delight to watch and to hear. She is truly one of the finest actresses we have in Scotland today, despite her tender years, and Alan Craig should be congratulated for bringing her talents to light. In this jaded critic's humble opinion, she is the next Bernhardt.

Claire quickly flipped ahead, reading snippets and snatches of reviews of plays she'd never heard of. Adrienne Auvergne — Ed's mother — had been the young leading lady of the company. Each review was filled with glowing comments about her performances, whether it was Shakespeare or some mild little contemporary comedy.

Ten pages later, Claire found what she was looking for — a picture of Adrienne from a program, the paper half-torn and yellowed with age. She was wearing a straw boater and a girlish white dress with puffy sleeves. She *was* beautiful.

But there was something odd about her. Claire couldn't quite place what it was, but she looked familiar. Where could she have seen that face before?

She started and jumped up, her eyes darting to the wooden figure across the room. Of course — that was Adrienne. She was the model for the mannequin. The resemblance was undeniable, from the delicate features to the hair to the elegant carriage of her head and shoulders. This lifeless wooden dummy *was* Adrienne. It was uncanny. And it was creepy.

Claire lifted the heavy book and put it aside. She tried the next one. This was 1960 and Adrienne looked even lovelier in her pictures. She had lost some of her juvenile cuteness and was maturing into a very beautiful young woman. The reviews were as praising as ever, and one mentioned the fact that the lighting designer (unnamed) seemed to compliment Adrienne's beauty in each scene, bathing her in rosy or radiant light.

More excited now, Claire rummaged through the old books until she found the one she wanted. She wasn't sure how old Ed was, but 18 was a pretty good guess, which would mean he'd been born in 1966.

And there, on the second page of the scrapbook, was the picture she needed. It was a group shot of the theater people, taken outside Blairmore on a sunny summer day. The moors were carpeted with heather, and some of the actors were lying around on it, taking their ease. The castle looked exactly as it did here in Becket, and even the gravel drive was the same. It was eerie to see this scene, so like what she saw each day, and yet, so unlike it at the same time.

The caption of the picture read, "Rehearsal for a Red-Letter Day. Leading lady Adrienne Auvergne with manager Alan Craig, surrounded by the Company. Her husband (lower left) holds Miss Auvergne's son."

She had her arm around a tall, dashing, mustachioed man in his late fifties, who had to be Craig. But she was smiling at the man in the lower left corner. It was Ben — nearly twenty years younger and very handsome, holding a baby in his arms. His clear brown eyes laughed up from the picture, focusing on the boy standing beside him. The boy was about eight and had a wild shock of sandy hair that partially obscured his face. Ryan! And of course that was Ed in his father's arms.

Claire marveled at the picture, holding up the heavy book to the light to get a better look. A piece of paper slid out of the back of the scrapbook, and she picked it up. It wasn't the same vintage as the book — this was a piece of Xerox paper. Claire unfolded it and read it carefully. It was a contract between Alan Craig and Sean Latham, giving Sean full managerial rights in perpetuity to Blairmore Castle and the theater company. It was dated Becket, Mass., 1980, and Sean had signed his name with a flourish.

Claire's mind was reeling with everything she'd just discovered. Now she understood —

the mannequin, especially. Ben's beautiful wife, whom he'd been unable to save in that fire, was now immortalized in wood. No wonder he didn't want to show her to anyone. This was his private tragedy, the hidden room in his heart that now housed his late wife and his memories.

Slowly, she closed the scrapbook and stood up, tentatively walking over to the dummy. She thought about Sean's lifetime contract. No wonder he had acted so strangely, had asked her to keep quiet. Alan Craig must have told him all about Ben, must have cautioned him what might happen in the future. But why would Sean protect the ventriloquist? Claire had an idea, a gruesome one, too. It wasn't just Ben who'd caused all these accidents. It couldn't be. He might be wacky and even a little mad, but there was a very sharp mind at work here as well. Claire was practically positive. Sean, creator of murder mysteries, director extraordinaire, the man whose credo was "the show must go on" — he was involved in this, too.

She left the inner room, extinguishing the bedside light, and touched the brass latch again to close the bookcase. Then, turning off the gas lamp in the library, she picked up her flashlight and started for the fake wall. She scanned the room again, verifying that everything looked just as it had when she walked in.

There was only one person who could fill in the final details, someone who'd been through it all. Ed was too young to remember, but Ryan could undoubtedly recall everything. She had to get him to talk.

CHAPTER
10

"**H**i," she said anxiously, walking into Ryan's office. He was studiously reading a giant catalogue with pictures of the latest lighting equipment.

"Claire! You're supposed to be in bed," he scolded, lifting his feet off the big oak desk. They were up above the shop in a cozy glass-enclosed warren filled with the items of his trade — inkies, pin spots, top hats, barn doors, and gels in all the primary colors.

"I was, but I'm not," she began. This was going to be hard. How did you ask someone if his father was a homicidal maniac? "It was just impossible to sleep and I feel really fine," she told him.

He nodded, and the silence between them hung heavy in the air.

"Can I talk to you?" Claire asked. "Really talk?"

He blushed, then lowered his head so she couldn't see the color in his cheeks. "I'm not

130

much on talk," he said. "It's about Ed? You got problems?"

"Well, we haven't been as close as we were," she acknowledged. "But that's only because he thinks I'm imagining everything. He's not a theater person, like we are, and he can't really appreciate what goes on here."

"What goes on. . . ." Ryan repeated. He looked confused and puzzled, also as though he wished she'd refrain from confiding her innermost secrets.

"Do you remember that room I told you about? On the way up the staircase to the tower?" She might as well blurt the whole thing out at once.

"I — yes, I remember," he said.

"I went up there again this morning and looked around."

He frowned and rubbed his forehead. "You did?"

"It's not just the female mannequin, Ryan; I found all the scrapbooks," Claire went on eagerly. "Reviews of shows and pictures of Blairmore years ago, when it was in Scotland — in the good old days, as your father would say." She waited for his reaction, but there was none. "There was a picture of you, too. You were about eight years old then."

"Oh?" He seemed mildly interested, but unconcerned.

"And Ben's holding Ed in the shot — he was just an infant. Ryan, am I right? Adrienne Auvergne, Ed's mom — she was the one Ben patterned that dummy after."

"Adrienne. . . ."

"Now listen," Claire rushed on. "I have this theory, and I don't think you're going to like it, but you've got to listen. I think Sean knows that your father's had some bad times, and maybe has been under a lot of pressure lately." She had to say this in the nicest way possible, so he wouldn't get mad. "Now for some reason, Sean doesn't want anyone else to know what's been going on at the theater. My theory is that Alan Craig paid Sean to keep a lot of things quiet. Like maybe what started the Blairmore fire in 1966." The ideas formed themselves even as the words spilled out of her.

"Claire, you're going to get yourself in too deep here," Ryan said hastily.

"Oh, Ryan, won't you help me?" she begged.

"There's no way to help. Not anymore." He was about to go on when the door to his office opened and Sean and Stephanie burst in.

"For Godsakes, Claire," Sean grumbled. "Can't I trust you for a moment? The doctor said you're supposed to stay in bed for three days. I talked to him."

"In bed," Stephanie added, "means lying down in a prone position, not running all over the theater."

"Yes, I know. I was just going back. Honest." She sighed and walked to the door, feeling like a small child who had just been sent to bed with no supper. If Ryan wouldn't help, she'd have to do this on her own. As for Ed, he was out of the question. Everytime she brought up the subject of his father, he crawled back into his shell like some kind of snail.

"I don't want to see your face again," Sean muttered. "No concert tonight, either." Monday, the night the theater was dark, was usually reserved for a trip to Tanglewood, the music festival in Lenox, which was a few towns over. "Mrs. McLeod will bring a tray to your room at suppertime."

"Sean —" she protested. He couldn't be serious!

"And if you won't stay put, I'm going to have to lock you in. Now get going."

He would, too. Because he had a stake in what was going on, and only Claire might spoil it.

On her way down the corridor toward her room, she saw Ben and stopped dead in her tracks. He was sitting in Mrs. McLeod's alcove, and the dummies, his constant companions, were lying near him.

"Hello, Claire," he said softly.

It never failed to amaze her, the way he could recognize footsteps. "Ben, hi. How're you doing?" She wanted it to sound casual, but it came out choked.

"I didn't know you were back from the hospital. I was worried."

I bet you were, she thought angrily. "I'm feeling fine, actually. Good as new. Probably the bop on my head did me some good."

He laughed, a slow, gentle laugh. "Better take it easy, even so. You never know how these things can catch up with you."

"Right. As a matter of fact, I'm on my way back to my room right now. Sean's orders." She realized even as she spoke that it was stupid to tell Ben any of this. He could *hear* where she was going; undoubtedly he could sense what she was thinking.

"Good idea. See you later. Are you going to the concert tonight?"

"I don't think so. I guess I'll make it an early night. You have fun, though."

"Thanks, I will. Got to get to work now, though. I'm trying to teach Howard to whistle." He stood up, taking the mannequins with him. "See you later, Claire."

She walked away briskly, letting her heels make a racket on the flagstones. Would he really go to Tanglewood, or would he hang around, just waiting for the opportunity to get her alone? One thing was sure — she didn't intend to do any snooping until she'd seen Ben Clark get into a car and drive away.

The day passed like molasses pouring. It seemed impossible to sit still and bide her time, so Claire gave up trying. About 5 P.M., she sneaked out of her room to get her gold heart from the dressing table. There was no one in the shop — work was finished for the day — so she didn't have to be too careful. But when she switched on the dressing room light and scanned the table, she was dismayed to see that the heart was missing.

"Did I take it with me to the hospital?" she murmured. "No, Maggie must have picked it up when she came to clean the costumes."

Claire looked around once more, but without result. The uneasy sensation she'd had so often in the past few weeks returned, and her palms were suddenly damp and clammy. "My good luck charm," she said, feeling more like Kim every moment.

She left the room and went to the phone in the shop, trying to recall exactly where she'd put the heart after the clasp broke. But by the time Claire got Ed on the phone, she realized it was useless. She'd have to forget about it until she saw Maggie.

"Hello. I'm back," she told Ed.

"You should have stayed in the hospital," he growled.

"Nice greeting. You talk like you're worried about me," she teased.

"Well, maybe I am."

"Maybe you should be. On the other hand," she paused, "I can take care of myself."

"Yeah, you've been doing a real swell job of that so far," he snapped.

"Ed —"

"I guess you're not going to Tanglewood tonight, in your condition. How'd you like some company?" he suggested, his voice softening.

"Oh, no!" She stopped, realizing how that sounded. She knew he'd never speak to her again if she told him she was going to spend the evening looking for evidence that would send his father to jail. "I mean, I'm going right to sleep after dinner. That is, after I wake up from the sleep I'm going to get right now."

"I could watch you," he said kindly. "I'd be your guardian angel."

"I'd like that," she responded dreamily. No one had ever talked to her like that before. It made her insides melt like a scoop of ice cream in the sun. "But if you were here I'd never sleep. Go on to the concert and have a good time. I'll see you tomorrow."

"Well, if that's how you want it, . . ." he agreed reluctantly.

"Not really. Understand?"

"Sure," he laughed. "Bye, Claire."

"Bye."

She looked at the black plastic receiver longingly, wishing she could get him back on the other end and make it all right between them. She had no idea when she'd really see him again, and that scared her.

And yet, cruel as it seemed, she knew she was doing the right thing. As soon as everyone had gone, as soon as she was sure that Ben and Sean were away from the theater, she would go upstairs to the hidden room and take the scrapbooks.

She crept back to her room and stayed there until dinner, just as Sean had instructed. She knew that if she disobeyed, he'd lock her in. Tonight of all nights, she couldn't risk that.

She chatted with Mrs. McLeod when she brought her tray, and asked what they were playing at Tanglewood that night. She was delighted to hear it was an all-Tchaikovsky program. If there was anything she loathed, it was Tchaikovsky. At last, when she feared she couldn't carry on the cheery act another minute, the old woman made her excuses and went down to her own dinner.

By seven o'clock, Claire was nearly climbing the walls. She peered out of a chink of a window in her room and anxiously waited for the truck to be brought around. The cast and crew trickled out; she counted heads. Good, there was Sean and Ryan. Bob came out with Stephanie, Charlie, and Mrs. McLeod. She bit her lip. Where was Ben? Finally, the ventriloquist appeared, nattily dressed in a maroon turtleneck and tweed jacket, but it occurred to Claire that he looked naked without his ever-present dummies.

She breathed a sigh of relief. The box-office staff came out, then the two techies who helped Bob with the heavy work. Everyone was accounted for.

She sat back on her bed, listening to the sounds of the voices, the motor starting up, and the truck doors opening and closing.

When she heard the vehicle drive away, Claire got up and went to the door. It was too bad that Ed wouldn't be with her — she felt sorry for him and sorry, too, that their budding relationship had been cut off by what had happened at the theater. Maybe once everything was back to normal. . . . But how selfish of her to think that way! Ed wasn't going to feel very romantically inclined toward the girl who had messed up his family life once and for all.

The hall was silent. She didn't bother to cover the sound of her racing feet as she sped toward the stairway and climbed to the top in record time. Claire pushed at the fake wall with every ounce of strength she possessed, then watched as it closed slowly behind her. The library looked just as it had the other day. She turned on the gaslight and went directly to the chink in the bookcase, pressing on the brass latch to open the wall of the hidden room.

The dummy was nowhere in sight. The dressing room was a shambles, the bedclothes in a heap on the floor, the knickknacks torn off the shelves as if someone in a fury had wanted to sweep away everything beautiful out of his sight. Some lay in chalky pieces, jeweled bits of enamel sparkling off the old Oriental rug. Claire was horrified, but not really surprised. Ben must have known — or sensed — that someone had been up here. He must have been panicked and furious to find his special hideaway disturbed. She would have to work quickly.

The scrapbooks lay on the dressing table where she had left them. Should she take just the top one, or all of them? He'd notice either way that something was missing. But wait a minute. . . . Would the books themselves actually be evidence of foul play at the theater? Probably not. She hadn't really thought of that. If she found the dummy, she could show from the pictures in the books that Adrienne Auvergne was the model for Ben's obsession, but that, in itself, was merely a point of interest. It didn't begin to explain his devastating anger, nor his penchant for trying to do away with ingenues, one after the other.

She sat down heavily at the dressing table,

stumped. "A fine sleuth you are," she told her reflection in the ornate Victorian mirror. "You don't even think before you jump in and put your fingerprints all over everything."

Yet she couldn't get over the suspicion that she didn't have all the facts, that she had put the wrong clues together in the wrong order. With fanatical studiousness, she began to read the books, starting with 1964. Here was a shot of Adrienne going hunting with Ben, Alan Craig, and several other company members. Here she was, posing in costume and makeup as Queen Elizabeth, surrounded by her male entourage. In every shot, Claire noticed, Adrienne was the only woman. Was this a coincidence, or did she have something against the competition?

Claire finished with that book and put it aside, picking up 1965. As she turned the pages, a picture of Adrienne began to form in her mind — a young girl, catapulted to the pinnacle of success in Scottish theater at such a tender age — hardly older than Claire herself. Granted, Scotland was very small potatoes compared to London, but Adrienne had all the time in the world to get where she wanted, or so she must have thought. The darling of Blairmore, worshipped by Alan Craig and courted by Ben — courted for years, according to the scrapbooks. They'd probably known each other for five seasons or so before he proposed, or before she said yes. Was she waiting around for a better offer, or perhaps for a better manager who might find just the right role for her on the glorious London stage?

Claire frowned down at the book, closed it, and picked up 1966. Maybe she was completely wrong about Adrienne. She might just as easily have been a lovely, unspoiled country girl with a thick Scottish burr and no pretensions at all. Perhaps she loved Ben dearly all that time, but Craig persuaded her to wait — for the sake of her career, or maybe because he was a little in love with her himself. Claire turned to that group shot again, the one with Ryan and Ed in it. The expression on Adrienne's face as she looked at her husband was filled with love and warmth.

Of course, it was possible that the real truth lay somewhere in between, or hidden away, just like the mannequin.

"This is no good. I'm not getting anywhere," Claire muttered. Suddenly, she looked up with a start. Had she heard something? No, only the hissing of the gas lamp. She kept going, turning the pages and hoping for the answer.

At last she came to a newspaper photo she had dreaded seeing. It was the castle in smoldering ruins against a stark sky. In the foreground, several cast members stood beside Alan Craig, who stared at the castle as though he had had lost his only child. There was a terrible feeling of desolation in the picture, as though, for all these people, it was truly the end of their world.

The newspaper account beneath the picture told Claire the details of the fatal fire that had changed so many lives. It had broken out just after a long Sunday rehearsal, and the flames had spread quickly. Adrienne and three other actresses had been trapped in their dressing room when the ceiling fell in; five crew members had perished in the shop, where the lengths of raw lumber had caught almost before anyone was aware there was a fire. The lighting director had been dragged out of the castle by a rescue team, but learning that his wife was still inside, he had lunged back into the flames to save her. He was far too late.

When he staggered back out again, his hair and half his face on fire, unable to see, he had been rushed to the local clinic. Unfortunately, he did not regain his eyesight. His two young sons, who had been in a far wing of the castle with the housekeeper, were unharmed. He subsequently took them out of the country — it was believed to America.

"The results of the investigation were conclusive," the article ended. "The cause of the fire was a faulty electrical system. There was no indication of arson."

Claire closed the book with a disgusted sigh. She had all the pieces, knew all the pertinent information, and yet none of it fit together. Ben's tragedy had taken place eighteen years ago, and for him, it was as though it had happened only yesterday. He had loved Adrienne desperately — enough to give his life for her. When he failed in his attempt to save her, he'd enshrined her in a dummy's body so that he could keep her memory alive forever.

But then, why would he want to tie her up? And why suddenly, this summer, would he have begun to lash out at other people like her and Kim? The other thing that puzzled her was Sean's connection to this. Craig had entrusted him with the castle and had probably insisted he hire Ben. But there had been no evidence of arson, so what could Sean be covering up for? All of it, she thought, had to do with Adrienne's personality. Whether she was an angel or a devil, she had Ben so ensnared in her clutches that he'd gone completely berserk. She had been the cause — unwitting or deliberate — of so much that was bad.

She was still sitting there when she heard a sound, the hollow ring of metal on stone. It came at regular intervals, and it was getting closer. Claire felt her insides tighten like steel bands. Where could she go to hide? How could she get her legs to move?

She pried herself away from the table and dashed back to the library where she extinguished the gaslight. Now she heard footsteps, the even pattern of a man's walk. Pulling the heavy bookcase after her, she retreated into the dressing room. The armoire — of course!

She opened the door and the musty odor of old clothes and mothballs assailed her. Taking a deep breath, she crouched down in the dark, thankful to have discovered some hiding place, no matter how small or cramped.

And then a terrible thought occurred to her. The first night she'd come to the library after hearing the voices, she hadn't been able to figure out how anyone could have gotten out of the dressing room. He'd been in here all the time — listening to her, watching her. The realization of that made her faint and dizzy.

The steps came closer. She was certainly not imagining them. But she'd seen everyone leave for the concert. No, that wasn't true. She'd listened to the truck pull away, but hadn't looked out the window. Which meant that he'd told the others he'd changed his mind and wasn't going after all. Which meant that he and Claire were alone together in Blairmore Castle.

The steps were almost on top of her. She heard the library wall open and close. The light sound of metal accompanying the footsteps suddenly made sense. She'd never seen Ben use a cane, but she'd heard that sound often enough on the streets back home. A blind person tapping a white cane before him as he walked.

Willing away the awful chill of fear that coursed through her, Claire made herself sit perfectly still in the closet. She glued her eye to the keyhole and waited. In a moment, she would know everything.

CHAPTER
11

CLAIRE thought herself small, then she concentrated on becoming invisible. He knew about this closet — he'd used it himself. Wouldn't this be the very first place he'd look? And why had she picked a hiding place with no means of escape? She was trapped like a rat in a hole.

The bookcase trembled and moved. Claire could imagine his fingers, groping for the brass latch, pressing it, sensing the movement of the heavy wall. She heard the cane tap, tapping inside the dressing room. Then it was flung aside.

The figure came into her line of vision. There he was, exactly as she'd seen him on the staircase, wearing his top hat and cape, the plastic mask over his face. Claire wanted to cry out, but her mouth was dry as a desert — and that saved her. Maybe he was just in some sort of trance. . . . Maybe if she called his name, he'd snap out of it and be fine again.

But could she risk that?

Keeping as still as she could, she watched him

walk to the bed, his hands groping the air. He bent down and pulled something from under the bedframe. His body obscured her view for a moment, but then he rose and turned toward her. In his arms was a short, black coffin, a child's coffin.

Claire couldn't breathe. She was choking, drowning in her own terror, but somehow, she forced herself to watch the scene that unfolded before her.

Snapping the side locks, he opened the coffin and, with a gentleness that seemed incongruous in this situation, he removed a small figure.

It was the mannequin, dressed in a sky-blue gown, her red hair gleaming in the dim light. She lay in his arms like a fragile bit of sky herself, something stolen from the clouds and moon and stars, some bit of beauty he could keep forever in his hidden room.

He lay her on the chaise, arranging her gown around her slight body as though she were a princess and he her faithful valet. Something on her neck sparkled in the light and caught Claire's attention. With a lurch of understanding, she reached up and touched her throat. The mannequin was wearing her gold heart on its seed-pearl chain!

She couldn't stop staring at it. That was her good luck charm that had carried her through so many awful events. But now, she had no control and she had no protection. She shivered, realizing that he'd taken the heart off her dressing-room table to give to the dummy, his beloved.

The masked figure bent over the mannequin and, before Claire's horrified eyes, he pulled a gleaming kitchen knife from beneath his cape. His breathing was ragged; each breath tore from his throat as though it pained him to inhale and exhale.

The high, silvery voice Claire had heard through the wall spoke. "It's only games," she heard the masked creature say. He didn't bother to throw his voice.

Then, in a deep growl, he responded, "Into the flames." He lifted the knife high and plunged it into the mannequin's wooden chest. Red spurted from it — a capsule of stage blood that he must have palmed — and the gold heart was stained with it. The crimson ooze covered the sky-blue bodice, turning it a rusty green.

He shrieked as though the knife had pierced his own heart and collapsed, moaning, over the wooden form. Claire saw them lying together, almost like two lovers, locked in a furtive embrace. She tried to close her eyes, to shut out the sight of this bizarre ritual murder, but it was impossible. She kept seeing the knife descending, over and over, kept hearing the awful shriek of agony.

At last, spent and exhausted, the murderer picked up his victim and deposited her in the coffin. He snapped the lid shut, picked it up and carried it out of the dressing room. He pulled the bookcase closed after him.

Claire waited a long time before she dared move. The minutes ticked by in her consciousness and once again, she relived the killing she had just witnessed. The man was sick, terribly sick, and needed help before he killed for real.

At last, stretching her cramped limbs, she half-stood and pushed open the door of the armoire. On shaking legs, she stepped out and closed the closet door. She couldn't stay here another minute — she felt unclean just standing in the room where so much horror had transpired.

She escaped from the room as though she were being chased. She paused once in the library to listen, but she was alone. Then, yanking at the false wall, she went through and jumped over the banister, back onto the rickety stairs. The old walls seemed to laugh at her, mocking her fear with their solid presence. Who did she think she was, they seemed to say, to think she could survive in the face of murder and madness?

She fled down the long corridors, past the actors' quarters, past Sean's office, and down the stairs toward the side entrance of the theater. She didn't breathe freely until she stood outside in the night air, panting and sobbing. She didn't know which was more dangerous, to stay or to run. But being alone with him in the castle seemed insane. He'd find her eventually — he could hear a footstep several rooms away and identify it.

Adrienne had become twisted in Ben's mind, a lovely dream that ended as a nightmare. And now, her power over him had caused him to perform that strange ritual murder. After what Claire had seen tonight, she couldn't keep quiet about it any longer. Sooner or later, the victim of his rage would be made of flesh and blood instead of wood and straw — and there was a very strong likelihood that the victim would be Claire herself. So she would have to take the chance. She was going to the police.

Bob's new used car was parked just down the gravel drive. He'd finally given in and made the seller an offer, and though he complained bitterly that he'd been taken, everyone knew that he was pretty pleased with the old heap. Because it was unthinkable that anyone would want to steal such a lemon, Bob always left the doors unlocked and the keys under the driver's seat.

Claire was running down the gravel as fast as she could. There was only a sliver of a moon, and the few stars that were visible were veiled with thick clouds. She could make it! She'd be long gone before he caught up with her. Her hands yanked at the rusted door handle and the car door flew open, creaking loudly as she pulled it ajar. Her fingers fumbled under the seat's moldy stuffing. Where were those keys?

With a gasp of relief, her hand closed around metal. She drew out the key ring and shakily inserted one of the bunch into the ignition. It didn't fit. Frantically, she tried two more, and in her haste, the second broke off, snapped neatly in half.

"Damn!" The tears sprang to her eyes and she swiped at them, looking back over her shoulder at the open door of the castle. It gaped at her, like a yawning chasm out of which anything might emerge, snarling and ravenous, at any moment. She pulled at the half-key, but it wouldn't budge. She stuck an edge of her fingernail in beside it for leverage, but that did nothing at all. At last she remembered the emery board she'd stuck in her jeans pocket that morning. She quickly withdrew it and shoved it into the spot, dislodging the key in an instant. Her finger was bleeding where the jagged metal had ripped it, but she had no time even to wipe the blood off.

The last key fit. She floored the gas pedal as she turned the key, crying with relief. The old car wheezed and coughed, but didn't catch. "Come *on!*" she urged it. "*Please!*" She tried again, pumping on the accelerator. It squeaked under her foot, but refused to behave. Why hadn't Bob bought a new car, for heaven's sake!

She sat back, biting her lips. She was simply too nervous, that's why it wouldn't work. Calmly, she tried it again. Nothing.

She glanced out the window at the blinking hint of starlight. It had seemed so kind and friendly on those nights when she'd sat with Ed on the parapet. That might have been a hundred years ago! If only he'd been able to listen, to take her side instead of his father's. But that was impossible. Claire thought of her own father, probably sitting in the den right now, watching television, or maybe writing her a letter.

This was no time to get nostalgic! Whatever it cost her, she'd have to go back inside that castle, get to a phone, and call the police. She'd lock herself in Sean's office until they arrived. She'd be perfectly safe there.

She ran, dreading her destination. Blairmore Castle towered over her, the shadow cast by its massive turrets swallowing her whole as she raced back inside. She kept her eyes fixed directly ahead of her, not daring to glance around. Sean's office was only a staircase and two corridors away.

Where was Ben? She prayed that he'd taken the coffin to some other wing of the castle, perhaps even gone outside himself to bury the gruesome thing. There was no way of knowing. He could be waiting for her around any corner.

No sound but that of her breathing and her footsteps. Just like hide-and-seek, just like that terrible game years ago where the two boys found her and locked her in the basement. Her father had saved her then — but who would save her now?

She was there. Her hand reached for the brass handle of the office door. The telephone was a yard away. She could feel it in her hand.

Her fingers were roughly torn off the knob and she cried out as she realized that he had found her. She was pulled away from the door, her body lifted and thrown down like a rag doll's. She forced herself to look up into those blank plastic features. He was strong, so strong that she knew she could never wrench free of him. The cape was tossed back over his shoulders; his massive arms pinned her to the floor.

"No, please! Ben, it's me!" she sobbed. "Don't hurt me. I'm a friend . . . a friend," she wailed, reaching up to rip the hideous mask from his face. The top hat fell sideways, revealing a wild shock of hair. He shrieked in terror and quickly grabbed for the mask, pushing it back in place, which momentarily gave her the edge. She shoved against him and scrambled to her feet, desperate to get away. But he was on top of her before she could stand, wrestling her back to the floor.

"Into the flames!" he hissed as he drew an old rag from the pocket of his tuxedo.

"Ben, *no!*" Claire gasped. The cloth came down over her mouth and nose, a foul odor emanating from it. It smelled of ammonia and size from the shop and something else, like the bottom of the swimming pool. Chlorophyll. *Chloroform*. She retched and tried to turn her head, but it was useless. Nausea hit like a rolling wave, carrying her along with it. Her limbs went weak, relaxed, and her body melted into a puddle at the madman's feet.

She didn't fight it anymore. She was unconscious.

CHAPTER
12

I N her dream, she was in front of the castle —
but it wasn't in America, she knew that. She
saw Adrienne walking out of the front gates,
ready for horseback riding, looking elegant in
her jodhpurs and hard hat. She was so beautiful,
so carefree. Claire tried to call her, but the
woman kept moving faster, her body becoming
more streamlined. She began to run, and then
Claire saw her body change. She sprouted a tail
and hooves, and then she became a horse, gal-
loping madly away while Claire pursued her.
Before the animal vanished, she turned her massive head. There were flecks of spit in the corners of her mouth, and her nostrils were flared
in anger. Claire called to her, but she kept going,
flying over the landscape.

Her mouth was dry, so dry. She thought of the
spit on the horse's mouth and licked her own
lips, but her tongue was parched, too. She
wanted to let her head loll back, but it seemed
impossible to manage that small a movement.
She could barely move a muscle.

"Ben," she murmured. Her eyelids fluttered open and she stared into the darkness. Still too tired to budge. . . . Maybe she should sleep some more.

She started, suddenly understanding that it wasn't exhaustion that kept her from getting up. Was it the drug — whatever was in that foul-smelling rag?

She was lying stretched out on her back and something made of metal was poking into her at intervals. Stretching her fingers, she groped for a handhold, but she couldn't move her arms. She was tied up! The thought hit her with frightening certainty. Her hands were bound to metal rungs on either side of her body, her ankles were tied together. A rope extended around her shoulders, across her chest and down through her legs.

"Oh, God," she moaned, bringing her head up as far as it would go. She was balanced precariously on some sort of ledge — she could feel a slight movement as she stirred, looking around. There was no floor beneath her, but the ceiling was so close she could have touched it if she could have gotten free. Where in God's name had he taken her?

She craned her neck, peering below her. With a sickening lurch, she closed her eyes. She was in the fly gallery over the stage, thirty feet up on the catwalk! The narrow ledge beside the lighting grid barely accommodated her slim body. Claire shuddered, tensing her muscles. She'd never had a fear of heights; indeed, had climbed right up here with Ryan her very first day at the theater. Now for some reason, she remembered the superstition she'd once heard that people who fall from a great height die before they land. Her head swam and the catwalk seemed to move beneath her.

Her palms were sweaty, too slick even to grasp the rungs on either side of her. "I'm all right, I'm not going to die. . . . I'm not going to fall," she said aloud to allay her fears. But the dizziness got worse — she was certain she was moving.

She licked her lips again, trying to think logically, to put panic in the back of her terrified mind so she could do something constructive about her situation. But it was impossible. All she could think of was that masked creature hovering over her, the smell of the rag, the strength in his powerful arms.

The ledge moved again, swaying like a porch swing. It seemed impossible to believe that she wouldn't fall, but her bonds kept her securely in place. There was a noise now, heavy boots climbing the iron ladder that led up the back of the stage to the grid. Claire's stomach turned over. He was coming to get her. What time was it now? Maybe nine at the latest. The concert wouldn't be over for another hour, and by that time. . . .

Desperately, she rubbed her wrists against the slate of the ledge, knowing even as the rusted bars cut into her soft skin that she couldn't possibly cut these ropes. The steps came closer, and got louder, the ring of boots on metal pounding in her ears. The ledge swayed, and stopped.

Claire was at the mercy of a crazed, blind killer,

a man who, despite his handicap, had a perfect sense of where he was at all times. He'd been a lighting director — he could undoubtedly negotiate the most precarious grid, even now. He would grope his way toward her and plunge a knife into her heart, even as he had with the dummy.

A head appeared over the top of the ladder. Claire blinked, unbelieving. Then tears of relief and joy sprang to her eyes.

"Ryan!" she sobbed. "Oh, thank God! I thought you were at the concert, that I was alone here with *him*."

Ryan stood there, staring at her, his hands clenching the ladder rungs.

"Come on, you've got to get me loose before he comes back! It's Ben, he got me up here somehow. Ryan, believe me — he needs help. We've got to find him. He killed the dummy of Adrienne and then he found me. He knocked me out and. . . . Oh, will you please get me loose!" She was babbling, panting, so happy to see him.

But he just stood there. "Claire," he said. "What is it? What did you see?" His voice was hollow and mechanical. It sounded so unlike him.

"That dummy," Claire sobbed. "The female dummy. It was your stepmother, Adrienne. Or at least it looked just like her. Oh Ryan, I know this sounds nuts, but your father killed it — or pretended he did. And it was wearing my gold heart — remember I told you I broke the clasp?

He must have taken it. I saw the whole thing. It was almost as if he wanted to turn Adrienne into me — to kill me!"

He drew his leg over the top of the ladder and crouched down, moving toward her slowly. "Adrienne's dead," he said in a whisper. "This time for good."

"What?"

"She never really died for him, you know. All those years, she had so much power over Ben — over all men — even after the fire. All those years, I had to listen to him talk about the good old days, but it was all her fault. It was like she died on purpose to spite him. He always loved my brother better than me, you know, because he was Adrienne's."

"Ryan, that's not true." Claire's heart banged around in her chest like a wild animal in a cage. Something was terribly wrong.

"It is true. It still is. He loved Adrienne better than me, so I had to kill her, don't you see?" His deep voice suddenly changed. "It's only games. . . ." The words came floating toward Claire in a high-pitched, silvery soprano. *Ryan — Ben taught him how to throw his voice.*

"Oh, God," Claire muttered. "Oh, no!"

"Into the flames!" Ryan intoned in his own voice. He pulled something out of his back pocket.

"Ryan, listen to me," Claire said in as level a tone as she could manage. But her blood turned cold when he reached for her and snapped the rope on her ankles with his mat knife.

"Now I've gotten rid of her for good. I'm free

of her and the power she had over him." He sawed at the ropes that held her arms.

"Please," Claire sobbed, the tears flowing down her white face.

Undoing the last of her bonds, Ryan quickly reached into his pocket again and drew out her gold heart on its seed-pearl chain. "You have to wear this now, just as she did," he told her solemnly, lacing it awkwardly around her neck. "You have to complete the circle." He lifted her in his powerful arms and held her high above the stage. Claire didn't want to look down, but she couldn't stop herself. She gasped when she saw the scenery of Sean's murder mystery below her, and way below that, the open trapdoor of the stage.

"Ryan," she made her voice hard and commanding. "Put me down now."

"But you saw me. You discovered my room and all my things, everything that meant so much to me. It was my world — mine and hers. But you spoiled it. Actresses!" He spat the word out. "They're all alike, all except her. You were the one who killed Adrienne. By finding out about her, by reading my scrapbooks and asking all those questions. That's why she was wearing your good-luck charm when she died. And now, you're wearing it again. Your good luck will send you out of this theater — for good. Out of my life and my brother's." He hoisted her over his head and she couldn't be brave anymore. She screamed once, and then shut her eyes, waiting for the end.

She heard someone calling. "Ryan, listen to me!" In her terror, Claire thought, she must be

157

hallucinating. It sounded exactly like Ed's voice.

"Ryan, everything's all right now. Put her down."

Claire couldn't believe her eyes when Ed clambered up onto the grid, scarcely looking where he was going as he edged closer to them.

"It's too late," Ryan hissed, his voice a deadly breeze through the ancient castle.

"It's not," Ed insisted. He didn't move any closer, but Claire could feel he was judging his distance from her. "You haven't done anything yet. You haven't hurt anyone, Ryan."

"I have. I killed Adrienne."

"Adrienne died a long time ago — you had nothing to do with that fire," Ed explained calmly. "You were only a child. Dad tried to save her, but he couldn't."

"I killed her."

"You killed a dummy, only a dummy. It wasn't a real woman." Ed was so patient, so perfectly self-assured. Claire listened to the hypnotic tone of his voice, and it somehow made her feel better. Then, she felt Ryan loosen his grasp on her, just a little. Was it enough? Or would she fall to her death anyway, unable to get her footing once she escaped from him?

"Adrienne loved him," Ryan said sadly. Then his voice turned hard. "Actresses, they're all alike," he repeated.

At that moment, Claire wrenched away, and in one leap she aimed straight for the big Klieglight that hung from the grid. Her fingers slipped, then caught. She embraced the cold metal shield with a sob of joy.

Ed moved as fast as she, thrusting himself in between her and his brother. Ryan's eyes opened wide, and then, like a child, he began to cry. Huge tears coursed down his face, but he made no attempt to wipe them away.

"It's okay, it's all right," Ed crooned, lacing his arms around Ryan to keep him from falling. He looked over to Claire and she just nodded, too shocked even to react. The two brothers clung to each other, perched high above the stage on the swinging grid.

"Can you make it down?" Ed asked Claire under his breath.

She exhaled, then tentatively stepped across, using the bank of hanging lights for balance. "Sure," she told him, although she only managed to get her limbs to move by sheer force of will. All she knew was, she had to get down, so she did.

Ed waited until she was on the fifth rung of the ladder and then he coaxed Ryan ahead of him. "Go on — you can do it," he encouraged his brother, who moved like a robot, planting one foot behind the other until finally, he stood on the stage floor. Ed jumped down beside him and then propelled him quickly across the stage, steering him out of Claire's line of vision.

"Wait here," he told her shortly.

She saw him take Ryan into the wings and then she heard them start down the backstage stairs.

Unable to stand up another moment, Claire collapsed on the set's sofa and rested her head heavily on the overstuffed cushions behind her.

She ran a trembling hand over her forehead and let it trail down toward her throat.

The gold heart! She grasped it tightly, suddenly realizing that the clasp was fine. Ryan had had it fixed for his dummy!

The irony and horror struck all at once and she began to laugh. She doubled over, the sick joke seeming hilariously funny under the circumstances.

"Hey, you, don't get hysterical on me." Ed was at her side before she knew it, his arms stealing around her.

"Oh, Ed!" she hiccupped. "I can't help it." She roared with laughter, unable to control herself, and let him wipe away the tears of mirth and fear and the whole crazy, awful experience. Then suddenly, she stopped. "Where is he?"

"Locked in the Green Room. I called the police from Sean's office." He hugged her tightly, desperately. "Oh, Claire, thank God you're all right. I never would have forgiven myself if I hadn't gotten here in time."

"But why did you?" She leaned back, looking into his brilliant blue eyes with affection and admiration. "How did you know to come to the theater at all? You told me you were going to Tanglewood."

"It was that phone call this afternoon. I knew when you didn't mention your suspicions once that you were planning something. All your nutsy talk about Ben really got to me — I started doubting my own convictions."

"I'm sorry about that — really I am," she said softly, reaching for his hand.

"I'd been looking the other way for so long, I had a lot of trouble seeing what was real. I never liked Ryan, the little I knew of him, so I just stayed out of his way whenever he was around, which wasn't too frequently. I wanted to forget all about him and my mother and his mother — and Ben, of course. I guess I didn't want to see what was right before my eyes, so I distanced myself from all of them. But you saw it. Ryan had a weird childhood, and I guess he never outgrew all those peculiar feelings he had about Adrienne, and by extension, all actresses, including Kim and you."

"You never talked to him about it, did you?" Claire asked.

"He never talked, period," Ed shrugged. "Who knew that he was fiercely jealous of anyone who took the attention away from him, like I did when I was born?" He shook his head. "I'm sorry you had to be the brunt of all his sickness."

"I wasn't really until I got Kim's part. When I was just the apprentice who wanted to act, he gave me a warning by locking me in that trap overnight. But when I actually got onstage, he let out all the stops."

"But he's been in the theater all his life. Why suddenly, this summer, would he flip out?"

"I guess he'd held in his hatred of Adrienne as long as he could. But over time, it festered and grew, until it finally exploded," Claire mused.

"That sounds logical. I never thought the guy capable of hate *or* love, as a matter of fact. He always seemed . . . I don't know . . . blank to me."

161

Claire shook her head. "I think he loved Adrienne terribly, though, in his own way. Why else would he have wanted to make a dummy that looked like her? She was all his up in that tower room, to do with as he pleased. Until I started snooping and found out about her."

"I'm glad you did. Maybe," he said with an embarrassed laugh, "maybe now I can make my peace with her, too."

He lifted Claire's chin gently and gazed at her with love and respect. "Thank you," he said simply. And then he kissed her. It was a long kiss, filled with a hundred emotions. When they finally broke apart, their faces remained close.

"Don't thank me," Claire said. "You saved my life, remember?"

"I think," Ed said as he drew her back into his arms, "we're even." Then they didn't say another word because they didn't have to. They understood each other perfectly.

CHAPTER
13

THE police arrived within twenty minutes. Luckily, Sheriff Granger knew Ed slightly from the times he'd written the police blotter for the *Bugle*. If he hadn't, it was highly unlikely that he would have believed the strange story these two kids told him. Ryan looked dazed as they brought him out of the castle to the squad car — Claire didn't know whether he actually remembered any of what had transpired that evening.

The police were about to drive off when the company truck rattled into the driveway.

"What the —?" Sean came barrelling toward them at a dead run, and Stephanie was right behind him. "What's going on?" he demanded. "Officer? Claire, what happened?"

"My half-brother almost killed Claire tonight," Ed told them brusquely. "He's the one who was responsible for all the accidents you've been having around here lately."

"What!" Stephanie went to Claire at once and

took her in her arms. "That's horrible. I can't believe it."

"I couldn't either," Claire began. But just then, she saw Bob help Ben down from the cab of the truck. She and Ed exchanged looks.

"Excuse me for a minute," Ed said. "I'd like to take care of this, if that's okay with everyone."

He walked steadily toward his father, his shoulders thrust back. Claire felt for him, knowing just what he had to be going through. She saw him approach the ventriloquist and gently take his hand. Then she turned away from the scene, sensing that what had to be said was for those two alone.

Sean talked to Sheriff Granger for a few moments, and then the police officer climbed into the car beside his partner. Ryan, alone in the backseat, looked stunned, as though he had no idea what was happening to him. They all watched in silence as the car drove away.

Claire shuddered slightly and looked back at the castle where so much had taken place. Now that it was over she was relieved, of course, but she was also grateful, aware that she had grown up as a result of all this.

"Your father will have a fit when he finds out," Sean grumbled, steering Claire back into the theater. Together they walked up the stairs and down the two corridors toward his office. "I never thought Ryan was wacko. Not at all. Actually," he said as they walked inside and sat together on the sofa, "I had it all wrong. I thought it was Ben."

Claire looked at him sharply and sat forward, facing him. "You *did* know something was going on. You wanted me to keep quiet about it."

Sean rubbed his moustache and then ran his hands over his face. He looked exhausted. "I'm ashamed to say you're right," he nodded. "When Alan Craig put me in charge of Blairmore five years ago, he told me Ben was part of the package. Living and working in this castle was his annuity, you see. No matter what he did, no matter whether he was able to work or not, he had room and board for the rest of his life. See, Alan felt he owed Ben a home. He was eaten with guilt over Ben's blindness and the death of his wife in that fire."

"Adrienne," Claire prompted him. "I know about her from the old scrapbooks in the hidden room."

"The what?" It was Sean's turn to look astounded.

Claire smiled knowingly. "I'll show it to you sometime. Ryan used it as a kind of . . . I don't know, a mausoleum, I guess you might call it. It's a long story." She shrugged when he looked at her questioningly. She got up, anxious to go and find Ed. But when she got to the door, she turned back to him. There was one more thing she had to know. "If you suspected Ben, why didn't you do something? I mean, I know you couldn't fire him, but you could have taken some precautions. Maybe that way, we'd have found out sooner that he was innocent. And someone else was responsible."

"You're right," Sean acknowledged, rising

from his desk and walking over to her. "I was too wrapped up in work to pay proper attention. That was pretty rotten of me, Claire. I feel lousy about it."

She nodded, accepting the hand he stretched out toward her.

"I'm going to talk to Ed and Ben, if that's okay," she said.

"Sure. Go on. Say, Claire," he called just as she stepped outside the door. "You will stay out the season, won't you? I mean, after all that's happened . . ."

"Are you kidding?" she grinned. "My parents are coming next week to see me star in your play. Sean," she shook her head at him, "didn't you ever hear the old saw, 'The show must go on'?" With a smile, she ran out of the room and down the hall. Where could Ben and Ed be, she wondered.

But before she got to the lobby, she saw them. They were sitting together in Mrs. McLeod's alcove, and Ed had his arms around his father.

Claire stopped where she was, feeling like an intruder.

"No," Ed said softly. "Come on over, Claire."

Ben raised his head as she approached, and she saw the tracks of fresh tears glistening on his face. She walked to him slowly and took both his hands in hers.

"Ben, I'm sorry."

"No, my dear," he said. "It is I who am sorry, that you should have been subjected to so much pain and trouble. There are more ways of being blind than we know," he sighed philosophically.

"I never wanted to see what had happened to Ryan."

She crouched beside him, looking at Ed, whose handsome face was filled with love and compassion for his father.

"I was selfish, you see," Ben said. "I had lost Adrienne, which to me meant that I had lost the world. More even than my sight and my job. Oh, she'd never had the time to be much of a mother to Ryan. It was hard for a little tyke around the theater, too. Adrienne was a delicate girl, a sweet darling whom Alan Craig carved into his image of a successful, brilliant, social butterfly. She didn't really want that life, but she respected him, listened to him. Almost more than she did me. But just before she gave birth to Ed, I convinced her to travel to America, to live there for a while. She'd agreed to take a leave from the theater. Ryan was so excited about that, you can't imagine. A new life, and a real mother for the first time in his life — someone to pay attention to him.

"But of course, once she was on her feet again after the baby, Craig put her back onstage. Just two months after Ed came, Craig had her wound in his tentacles all over again. She refused to leave Blairmore. Ryan suddenly started to change. He wouldn't eat and barely slept; he wouldn't play with the other children. And then, there was the fire."

Claire shook her head. "It must have been awful for him."

"Ah, yes," Ben agreed. "He didn't cry over her — no, he was furious. It was a terrible, cold fury, as if she had died on purpose to spite him."

Claire blinked as she remembered Ryan's words. He had said exactly the same thing, but had attributed the feelings to his father, not to himself.

"He still remembered his own mother running off, you see," Ben went on, "and he equated the two women. In his mind, they were both traitors."

Ed was silent, watching his father. Claire could tell how his own feelings had blossomed in this brief period of time, just by looking at his face. That restrained, tight expression he sometimes wore was gone.

"When we got to America," Ben continued, "I concentrated on my career. I was thankful that the Beckmans could take Ed, and therefore I was able to take Ryan all round the country with me. He was hardly in one school when I'd take him off again, and he rarely formed friendships, but he never complained, so I was able to convince myself that all was well. He seemed to enjoy the life, or so I imagined. I was distraught, you see, not thinking, trying so hard to adjust to life without vision, and without Adrienne. I took better care of Howard and Boko than I did of my sons, more's the pity."

Claire touched his shoulder gently, sad to see this self-hatred in him. It was understandable, of course, that he should feel this way. She hoped, in time, that he'd leave it behind him. "The dummy of Adrienne that Ryan kept up in the tower room — was that yours?" she asked him.

"Ed told me about that. No, I never saw it," Ben said. "He must have been obsessed with her, to have done something like that. When I taught him to throw his voice, to work with the mannequins, I never realized how he would use that knowledge." He took a deep breath and stood up. "If you two don't mind," he said, "it's been an awful night. I must get some sleep."

"Of course, Ben," Claire said.

Ed rose with his father and walked halfway down the corridor with him. "See you tomorrow, Dad?" he asked.

Ben's face broke into a peaceful smile. "I'd be delighted." He walked away from them, as always, his step sure and brisk. Ed just stood there, but Claire could tell his thoughts were racing.

"Dad?" Ed rushed toward him suddenly.

The two men faced each other and then, Ed put his arms around his father. They embraced fiercely, clinging to each other with all the love denied them for all those years. It seemed clear that they'd reached a new understanding together, one they would cherish for the rest of their lives.

Ben separated from Ed slowly, his face positively beatific. He had lost one son that night, Claire realized, but he had found another.

"Let's take a walk," Ed suggested when his father had turned the corner. He pulled Claire to him so they could walk hip to hip, and together they walked out through the lobby and into the night. The evening was mild — perfect for strolling.

"You must be quite an actress," Ed said at last.

"Well, sure," she grinned. "I am."

"Not onstage. I mean in real life, not to let on how scared you were." He shook his head. "When I think about what Ryan might have done. . . ."

"I *did* let on," she protested. "You just weren't listening very hard." She turned to him, her brown eyes glistening. "If it were my family," she said softly, "I wouldn't have listened either."

"I was an idiot, playing dumb like that," Ed countered. "You know, the weird thing is that I did some investigating myself. You turned out to be a lot better at it than I was, though."

Claire stopped and turned in the circle of his arms. "What do you mean?"

"Remember when Kim broke her leg, the first night you played the part, when I wouldn't come to see you?"

"How could I forget?" she said sarcastically.

"Yeah, well, it was for a good reason. I'd convinced Mrs. Krieling, the town librarian, to show me some back issues of the paper, farther back than what we keep in the office. After what I read about Alan Craig, and how he willed Sean the theater in perpetuity, I got even more confused. I thought maybe Sean was up to something, but I just couldn't figure out what he'd have against you or Kim. It never occurred to me when Ryan said he hated actresses what he really meant. Anyhow, I gave up on my investigation. I'm just glad that you didn't."

"I never would have figured it was Ryan," Claire told him truthfully.

"I'd like to see those scrapbooks now, Claire.

170

I can start to make sense of my own past, and where I came from. Will you take me to the hidden room?"

"Tomorrow," she nodded. "In broad daylight. I don't think I could face it right now."

"I don't blame you. Maybe we should take Ben up with us."

"That's a great idea," Claire nodded. "I'm really sorry I ever suspected him. I feel awful about it."

"Hey, it was logical. I guess Ryan dressed up like him to try to take his place, in a way. And for the same reason, he put your heart on Adrienne's dummy before he killed her. Nothing was what it appeared to be."

Claire smiled. "Like my father's always saying, the theater is all illusion."

"He's right, of course," Ed teased. "But only because he's your father," he added with a laugh.

"What about yours?" she asked suddenly.

Ed's face changed and softened. "It's weird," he said. "All those years, I kept telling myself that it didn't matter, that family wasn't important. But now I know I've got a father. A pretty terrific one, too. It'll be nice to get to know him after all this time."

Claire reached up and touched his face softly. "I'm glad to hear you say that."

"Thanks to you." Ed smiled, leading her on around the side of the theater. They nearly stumbled over a ladder that Bob had propped up outside the shop door. Claire quickly steered Ed away from it.

"What's the matter?" he asked.

"I'm not walking under that thing, and neither are you," she stated emphatically. "There's been enough bad luck around here to last us both a couple of lifetimes." She touched the gold heart at her throat as an extra added precaution.

"Don't tell me you've picked up that superstitious junk!" Ed laughed.

"I certainly have," she said adamantly. "And don't you dare make fun of it."

"Okay! All right!" He raised his hands in mock surrender. "But I'm feeling very lucky right now, ladder or no."

He pulled her to him and kissed her in the shadow of the castle, which now seemed a benign presence, not the threatening menace it had been only a few hours ago. It would have been hard for any outsider to tell that Blairmore had been the scene of so many awful occurrences, but not Claire. As she leaned back from Ed's embrace, she smiled up at Blairmore. The silent stones remained impassive, hovering over the young couple as if they, too, were part of its secret. Then the clouds parted and the thin moon appeared, beaming down on them like a blessing.